The Adventures of Beddigan T. Mouze

Volume 1

Mandy Lambert

Curved Bridge Books

ISBN 978-1-7750974-0-2

Original cover art: Jamie Heise
Original map art: Brian Patterson

Published by Curved Bridge Books

For the Blue Dragon who lives under the curved bridge, you will forever fire my imagination.

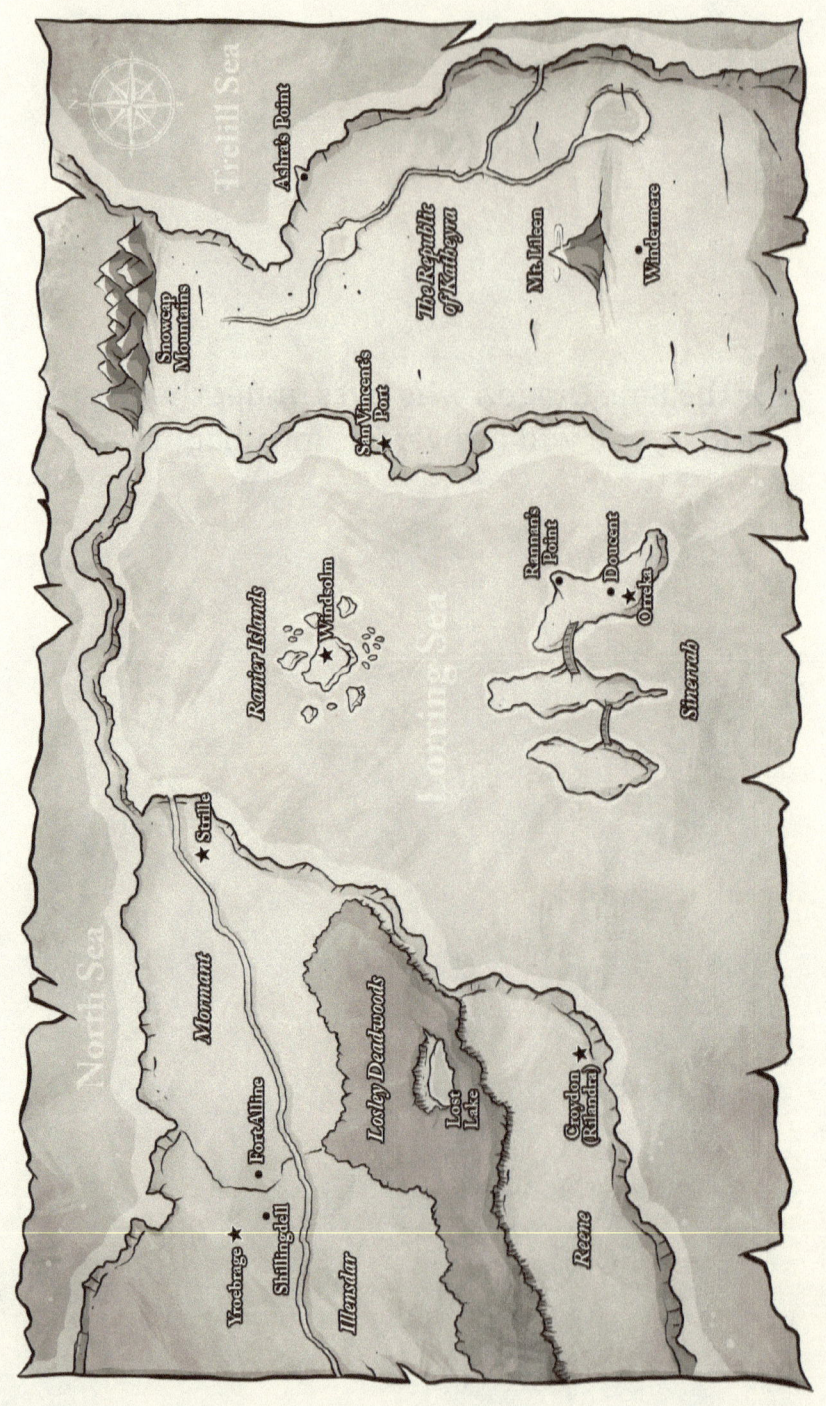

Chapter 1: Beddigan T. Mouze

The wind ruffled Beddigan's fur as he crouched against the smooth rock- face, his eyes never leaving the inky dark mouth of the cave. Moments before, the lumbering bulk of the famed red Dragon, named Galantus by the residents of the nearby village of Windermere, had landed on the bluff and stalked into its home. Little did the Dragon know that Beddigan T. Mouze had already been inside the cave and set a trap to finally rid Windermere of the vile, winged beast. One paw on the hilt of his sword, Beddigan crouched, frozen like a statue, waiting for the boom of the triggered explosion and the howl of the Dragon.

Time passed. Too much time. Straightening, he stepped cautiously towards the cave, brow furrowed. By now, he should have been well on his way down the mountain to collect his fee from the thankful villagers of Windermere.

Creeping towards the cave, he kept his ears perked for any sound of movement. Silence. Stifling a growl, he pulled out his illumination crystal from his pocket and affixed it to the leather gauntlet that wrapped around his paw and covered the bulk of his forearm. Tapping the crystal gently, he waited until the soft glow of green light penetrated the edge of the darkness of the cave. Moving slowly, he approached the darkness and peered inside, wincing when the leather of his boots creaked softly. He scolded himself inwardly for not having oiled them properly after his last adventure.

After a few steps into the cave the hulking form of the slumbering Dragon appeared in the faint glow of his illumination crystal. The iridescent scales of the beast shimmered and glowed as if lit from within. Beddigan froze, extinguishing the light and plunging them both into darkness, for fear of waking Galantus. He stood stiffly, paw firmly on the hilt of his sword, as he waited for any sign that the Dragon would wake. After a long stretch in the darkness, he tapped the crystal back on and crept behind a spire of rock, feeling confident that he had not woken the beast.

From this new angle, he could no longer see the Dragon's face. When Galantus had lain down he must have narrowly missed the triggers for the carefully packed and placed explosive crystals that Beddigan had set.

Stepping around the spire, he squinted, searching until he saw the tiny pink telltale marks of the explosives near the Dragon's tail, foot, and neck.

Beddigan's lip curled in a silent snarl of frustration. It should have been an easy end to this adventure. It had taken him time and coin of his own to put together the plan that would earn him enough gold to take a nice, long vacation. An explosion, a Dragon buried in rubble, and him with his feet up and a few tankards of ale, counting out his fee gleefully.

Extinguishing the light again, he moved quickly out of the cave, blinking in the bright sunlight as his eyes adjusted.

"Okay Beddigan... what in this Warbler's Cursed world do you do now?!" He snarled quietly, pacing around on the bluff. He angrily kicked a rock off the edge of the ledge and listened while it tinked and thunked down the mountain slope. His eyes settled on a much larger rock, this one about the size of his fist, and an idea was born.

He picked up the small boulder and tested its weight. It would be risky. He would have only one shot. It was dangerous. Even if it worked, the chances of being caught in the explosion were much higher this way. It either worked, or he ended up on the business end of a very angry Dragon, who undoubtedly would enjoy eating Mouse-flesh.

Beddigan turned towards the cave, gripping the rock tightly, "May Annilose watch over me," he muttered the prayer, stepping into the mouth of the cave. He closed his eyes, listening to the Dragon's heavy breathing. The smell of smoke tickled his whiskers. He visualized where he was in relation to the undetonated explosive crystals. Tucking the rock into the crook of his arm, he carefully loosened his illumination crystal from his gauntlet. Taking a deep breath, he activated the crystal to its brightest setting and tossed it into the cave, praying it would provide enough light for him to see his target. Eyes locking on a pink flicker, Beddigan heaved the rock into the cave, just as Galantus began to stir from the light, its massive head whipping around; golden eyes locked on him.

Beddigan leapt to the side, trying to escape the mouth of the cave as the explosion shook the mountain, and the Dragon roared. Rock exploded off of the cliff face as the other explosive crystals triggered. Beddigan tucked himself into a ball and covered his head and neck with his arms, waiting for the explosions to stop. He waited several minutes after silence descended on the mountain before lifting his head. Standing and shaking the rubble from his body, he crept towards the mouth of the cave. Huge slabs of sandstone, broken and jagged, filled the entryway of the cave completely. He leaned forward and listened carefully for any sounds of life within.

After a few moments he stepped away, looking out over the thick, evergreen forest below, towards the little village of Windermere, with its brightly coloured roofs. With a satisfying grin he thought, *I can officially add Dragon slayer to my resume*, as he started to make his way down the mountain.

***

Later that evening, after being greeted by the thankful villagers of Windermere and meeting with the town elders to claim his fee, Beddigan sat at a small table in the corner of the lively Three-Headed Rabbit Inn. He would always have a free room, a full glass, and a heaping plate of food in Windermere. The Dragon had slaughtered half of the town's population over the past turning, since it had taken up residence in the bluffs of Mount Lileen.

Dragons were rare in this part of the world, and few were skilled or crazy enough to try and slay one. The villagers thought it a thing of fate that Beddigan had shown up and taken on the task of ridding them of Galantus. But Beddigan had heard word of the Dragon while adventuring to the north. With the confidence that he could outsmart the Dragon, and the desire for the coin he would get for such a deed, he was immediately interested. But most of all, the challenge of such an adventure lifted his soul and set his blood afire.

So, he had made his way south, stopping in the bustling metropolis of San Vincent's Port to procure the crystals he would need for his plan. It had cost him a considerable amount of coin, but the fee for slaying the Dragon would more than make up for it. He had enough coin now to take a nice, long vacation, which he was desperately in need of. He had been on a steady streak of adventures for the past five turnings. Constantly, one job after another, creating quite the name for himself in this part of the world; and racking up quite the list of enemies as well.

He was starting to slip up with little things, like oiling his boots properly, or having a solid Plan B, simply due to exhaustion. But at the same time, he didn't have much desire for down time. He wasn't the type to lie on a beach or stay in the city for theatre and parties. He was happiest when he was adventuring; solving problems, battling beasts, saving fair maidens. He felt most alive when he had his sword in paw, battling for his life.

A pang of grief struck his chest at the thought of battles, and the memories of war, almost enough to make him set his tankard of ale down. He quickly chugged the remaining liquid, relishing the warm flush it brought on, trying to drown the feelings of unease, the thoughts of his time in Her Majesty's Royal Sapphire Brigade.

From childhood, he had wanted to be a soldier. Just like his papa and his uncles, and nearly every man in the Mouze family. He had paid attention in school, just enough to pass his subjects, until he was old enough to join Her Majesty's Royal Cadets. The fighting between his home country of Illensdar and the neighbouring kingdom of Mormant had been alive for ages.

He had lost papa to the very same war he would grow to fight in, many turnings later. Mama had begged him not to go to war, never having been the same once papa died. But more than anything in the world, he knew he must.

Thinking about mama always brought a tear to his eye, which he quickly blinked away. He had left mama, his little sister Clottie, and old uncle Thomas at their family homestead in Shillingdell and had made his way to the capital city of Yroebrage. The next six turnings of his life were spent training and battling in the name of Her Majesty, Queen Elendie.

He had worked his way up through the ranks of the army until he had been chosen to be a part of an elite group of warriors known as the Royal Sapphire Brigade. His time amongst those fine Mice were some of the best in his memory; and also some of the worst. He had made some great friends during that time, including Sir Charrin, who had been his most trusted friend and ally.

Beddigan signaled to the barmaid for another tankard of ale, while his mind flew unbidden into memories he had tried so very hard to bury. The shame of them caused him to hunch down in his seat, and to keep his eyes averted from the barmaid's as she delivered his drink.

Beddigan shook his head, trying to lose the image of betrayal that had been stamped upon Sir Charrin's face as he took his last breath. Beddigan's paw shook at the memory of sneaking away from the castle in the dead of night, knowing he could never return.

Slugging down more ale, he forced his mind to turn away from such thoughts, as he had trained himself to do over the turnings since he left his homeland. He was good at burying things. And running. And never letting anyone get too close. Pulling his coin pouch loose from his belt he started methodically counting the pieces, his ritual to bring himself back to the present.

Soon, having finished his last tankard of ale for the evening, he pushed back from the table and stretched, the room spinning a bit from his impairment. He started to move towards the stairs that would lead him to his room when he felt it: that feeling that someone was watching him. His paw instinctively moved to the hilt of his sword, as he sharpened his gaze and peered around the busy, raucous room. Nothing stood out as odd behavior among the many inebriated patrons. Chalking it up to the ale and haunting memories, he continued to make his way upstairs.

Fumbling with the key at his door he almost didn't hear the small voice behind him, "Excuse me, Sir. Are you Beddigan T. Mouze? The Adventurer?"

His back stiffened a bit, listening carefully before turning. A child's voice. He turned slowly and saw a little Mouse, no more than eight or nine turnings old, in a tattered pink dress. Her soft gray fur tufted along her cheeks. She stood a few steps away, tugging shyly on the hem of her skirt.

Beddigan tried to smile, though he was sure it came off as weak, and crouched down, holding out his paw, "Indeed I am, little one. How can I help you?" he asked.

The little Mouse stepped forward, reaching out to gingerly touch his paw, "It's.. I-It's my papa. And my village," she said with a sniffle. Her mouth quivered, "This a-awful beast came and took papa away. He has taken lots of papas and they say... they say he may come for the children next."

A door in the hallway opened before Beddigan could answer,

and a tall, striking lady Mouse is a rose-pink dress came out, startled to find them together in the hall. Her amber eyes softened when they settled on the child's distraught face, "Beatrice," the Mouse scolded softly, crouching down and pulling the little girl away from Beddigan, "I told you not to bother him. Go in, go to bed." She pushed the little girl towards the room she had come from.

Standing, she smoothed her dress, looking at Beddigan as he rose, "I am so sorry. I was going to approach you about helping our village in the morning. She must have been spying on you."

Beddigan smiled, genuinely this time, "It's alright. I take it you are her mother? And your husband was taken by some beast?"

Tears filled the Mouse's eyes, but she blinked them away furiously, "Yes, we need help in the worst way, which is why Beatrice and I came to see if you could help. You rescued my sister's village a few turnings ago. And we heard you were to take on the Dragon here."

Beddigan nodded along, but before he could answer, Beatrice burst from the room and wrapped her arms around his legs. "P-please mister Beddigan. I need my papa." She sobbed, while her mother tried to tug her away.

Beddigan crouched down, hugging the little girl close for a moment and then pushing her back into her mother's arms, "Don't worry, we will find your papa. Now do as mother says and go to sleep."

Beatrice sniffled and rubbed her eyes and headed back into the room. He heard her mother assure her that she would be right in before she pulled the door closed with a soft click.

Turning back to Beddigan, fresh tears in her eyes the Mouse asked, "Do you mean it? You'll help us?"

Beddigan nodded and reached to take her paw, "How could I say no?" he murmured.

They made plans to meet in the morning over breakfast downstairs, and Beddigan finally made it into his room, and shut the door. "So much for a vacation," he muttered, before collapsing on the bed.

Chapter 2: A Fox In Wolves Clothing

A large paw clamped down on Beddigan's shoulder, stirring him from his daydream. He sat at a small table in the Wicked Mule Ale House, having arrived in the Republic of Katheyra's capital city of San Vincent's Port two nights prior, after receiving a message requesting his services immediately. He had initially ignored the message, having already agreed to assist a small coastal town near the Snowcap mountains. However, there was something about the request; the lack of details, the haste with which it had been written, and, of course, the large sum that was promised, that caused Beddigan to draft a message to the town of Ashra's Point, advising them he would be delayed in his arrival.

"Well well well, looks as though you got my message, old friend!" A Bear of great size and even greater girth, boomed, as Beddigan turned to see the owner of the paw on his shoulder.

A grin spread across Beddigan's face as he rose and embraced the giant Bear, "William Bearhelm, in the flesh! My good friend, it is a pleasure as always. What's it been now? Two... no three turnings!"

The Bear returned his smile, dragging out a chair that looked as if it would barely hold his weight. Once settled, he signaled to the barmaid for a round of ale, "Aye, closer to the latter I believe. I've kept up on your tales though. Impossible not to with the way they talk of you," the Bear grumbled, accepting his tankard of ale from the barmaid with a wink.

Beddigan reclined in this chair, sipping his ale, a crooked grin tugging up the corners of his mouth, "Is that jealousy I hear, William?"

The Bear's fists slammed down on the table with a roar of laughter, sloshing ale over the rim of his tankard, "How could I not be at least a bit jealous when I hear my old friend has taken down a great Dragon *by himself*!"

Beddigan laughed as well, though much more softly, "It was a bit dicey at the end, but I got the job done. I have heard a bit of your tales as well, though nothing for the better part of a turning. What have you been up to, William, that has kept news of you so silent?"

The smile faded from his friend's face, "Ah well, a little of this... a little of that. Nothing too noteworthy..." the Bear said hastily, his voice much softer now.

Beddigan watched his friend's face carefully, noticing the nervous twitch in his right eyelid. He felt the drumming of the Bear's claws against the tabletop, and the shaking of his leg against the wooden table.

"Seems a bit more to it than that, William. Why did you bring me here? What's going on?" he asked, leaning forward and resting his elbows on the tabletop.

With a sigh that sounded much like a growl, William leaned

forward in his chair, resting his arms on the little table as well, which creaked under the added weight, "I've made some work as a sell-sword this last turning," the Bear said reluctantly. "Now, before you start in on me, I know it wasn't the best decision, but I had my reasons!"

Beddigan's face lost all manner of kindness as he stood abruptly, pushing back from the table, "I've nothing to offer you then. You know where I stand on mercenary work, William. It was nice to see you." And with that he moved away from the table, across the raucous room, towards the door. Stepping out into the cold night air, Beddigan sighed, feeling the ground rumble beneath his boots.

William exploded out the swinging door behind him, almost toppling him over, "Wait, Beddigan! I wouldn't have called for you unless it were desperate times. I need your help."

Beddigan turned on his boot heel sharply, "Do you not remember what happened, William? Did you conveniently forget why I loathe mercenaries?" he snarled, turning away again to stride across the open space that circled the Ale House.

A huge paw snagged his arm, holding him in place, "Annalose and Ardra, Beddigan!" William cursed, "Listen to me for one Warbler's Cursed moment!" the Bear roared.

He shook free of his friend's grasp and took a couple of measured breaths before turning around to face the Bear, crossing his clench-fisted arms across his chest. The light from the windows of the Ale House illuminated his friend's face; allowing him to see the fear in the Bear's eyes, "What have you gotten yourself into?"

William sighed heavily, "I am in a world of trouble, Beddigan," he paused a moment to look up at the sky, closing his eyes in the cool night air, "As I said, I took on some sell-sword work, most recently... in Mormant."

Beddigan's eyes widened with shock. The Kingdom of Mormant, the country bordering and at war with his homeland of Illensdar, far across the Lorring Sea, was one of strict military rule. Governed with an iron fist, the Wolves of Mormant were raised to believe they were next to Gods upon the world and therefore should be the rulers of all the lands. The long-past war between Mormant and the southwestern country of Reene had resulted in not only the complete subjugation of the Reenal Foxes under the heel of the King of Mormant, but also the destruction of over half of the country's land.

The Losley Deadwoods sat as a great scar upon the land that separated both Mormant and Illensdar from Reene. Few dared cross the eerie land, with its towering trees, hazy mist, and burned, ruined edges of forest; with stories of beasts, unknown to the rest of the world, inhabiting the ravaged place.

Instead, those with cause to travel to Reene chose to go by ship, further removing the country from the rest of the lands and helping to secure Mormant's hold upon it.

What was left standing of Reene was sparsely inhabited as the Mormant armies had all but exterminated the species and put into effect strict population control practices for the Foxes. Few countries had any business with Reene, with one exception: William's home country of Sinerrah.

"*Mormant?!* You signed on as a sell-sword for those monsters?" Beddigan bellowed.

William winced, shrugging his shoulders apologetically, looking cowed, "I didn't at first, but the coin was too great... I just couldn't refuse. Things have been rough back home for

Elenya and the kids. Erikkson has been ill for the better part of two turnings now, and you know healers don't come cheap, Beddigan. I was desperate."

Beddigan shook his head, frustrated, "Desperation leads to many things, William, stupidity obviously being one of them, but Mormant? *Mormant?!*" He began to pace, "They nearly cleansed a species from the land and if they had their way, my people and my country would follow quickly in Reene's charred footsteps."

Before William could respond, Beddigan rushed on angrily, "It's bad enough you were doing mercenary work at all. You know how often I clean up the messes left by mercenaries? Of course you do! You used to do that work as well. *We* did that work *together*. And yet, you sign on for that kind of ruthless job again? Did you fight my people? *How many Mice did you kill, William?*" Turning, he shoved at William furiously, grabbing fistfuls of the Bear's tunic and pulling his great bulk down to look into his eyes, "It could have been Clottie. *You could have killed her in a raid on a village.* You are no better than the thrice Warbler's Cursed fiends who killed Mama."

Releasing his grip on William's tunic he pushed his friend away, turning and stalking away a few steps, unable to look at the Bear.

William let out an anguished snarl, "I know Beddigan. I *know!*" William buried his face in his paws, "I didn't take any work in Illensdar. I could never do that after being your friend all these years. We were down in Reene, controlling the rebellion."

Beddigan snorted in disgust, "Thanks. Good to know you have my back," he said dryly.

William snarled, "Look, Beddigan, we can't all be heroes,

swinging in and rescuing maidens and defeating Dragons. I have a family to support. I know that what Mormant did to Reene is a terrible, awful thing, but what's done is done. If not me, some other Bear would take the work and my family needed the coin. I did what I had to do, which *you* of all people should understand!"

Beddigan let out a sharp bark of sardonic laughter, as the shame he felt at his friend's words stabbed into his gut, "Rationalizing may help you sleep at night, but I know better of it."

William roared in frustration, scooping up a rock from the side of the dirt path and hurling it into the woods.

Beddigan leaned against a tree, bent over with paws braced on his thighs, breathing deeply to regain his composure. "If you needed coin, you could have asked," he spoke quietly to his friend, who had followed suit and was now leaning against a tree which bowed backwards under his mass.

"I am not a charity case," Wiliam responded stiffly.

Beddigan bit back another sharp reply, choosing not to speak it, lest it thrust them back into a shouting match. The silence stretched between them.

William shifted and Beddigan felt his friend's eyes on him, "Beddigan, look at me. Please." Beddigan straightened against the tree, turning to face his friend. "I need your help. The Wolf I had been working for, Commander Rollstad, did not take kindly to my severing our working relationship. Believe it or not, I didn't enjoy the work. I won't call it a mistake because it got Erikkson the help he needed, but as soon as I could step away, I did."

Beddigan nodded, squelching the anger that leapt up at even hearing the name of the notoriously cruel Mormant military leader. His time in Her Majesty's Sapphire Brigade had served only to increase his distaste for the enemy nation of his homeland.

"I was privy to some sensitive information in my time under his command," William continued, "and being the only sell-sword in the contingent, I gather I wasn't ever meant to leave alive."

Beddigan stiffened, "There's a price on your head?" He asked, paw instinctively dropping to the hilt of his sword. Beddigan was suddenly aware of how weary William looked. The whites of the Bear's eyes were yellowed by exhaustion, his tunic torn and ratty around the edges. The leather of his boots and belt were cracked and worn.

"Aye, there is. I used an alias as you taught me, but I fear for Elenya and the kids. Sinerrah is as safe a place as any, but Mormant is a powerful country to have as an enemy, especially that Commander Rollstad."

Exhausted, William slumped to the ground, leaning against the tree, "I've been running; evading them for too long. I'm bound to slip up eventually, and they will be there when I do." His eyes looked up, searching to meet Beddigan's, "I know I messed up. I know I brought this upon myself, but I really need your help, Beddigan. You are the only one that I can trust."

Beddigan nodded stiffly, "Name it," he murmured, mind already racing ahead to how he could possibly make enough coin to potentially buy off the Commander or one of the would-be assassins on his friend's tail.

The silence stretched between them again until William broke it with a sigh, "I need to know how you did it all those years ago. I need you to make me disappear."

***

Beddigan awoke with a start, at a loud crash just outside the door of his room at the Wanderling's Inn, near the south wall of San Vincent's Port. Leaping out of bed he flung the door open, paw gripping the hilt of his sword. The door next to his own, the room William had been sleeping in, was cracked down the middle and dangling off of its hinges. William was just inside the door, leaning heavily on the door jamb, panting; eyes feral, and teeth bared in a wicked snarl.

Beddigan released the hilt of his sword and cautiously approached his friend, "William? Are you hurt?" he asked, carefully stepping closer to his friend.

The Bear's breathing slowed, returning to normal, and he blew out a long breath, his hulking shoulders shaking from the released strain, "I'm fine. I just... I was certain someone was trying to break into my room. No one around though," the Bear muttered.

Beddigan looked around the corridor, which was empty except for them, despite the racket his friend had made in the wee hours of the morning. *Typical Katheyran's*, he thought, as the Badgers of this land were well known to mind their own business, often to a fault.

The stairs creaked and Beddigan's paw flew to his sword again, just as the barkeep and owner of the Inn's head peeked up at them.

The Badger's beady eyes darted around the scene; the cracked and broken door, the still shaking Bear, and Beddigan himself, naked except for his breeches, ready to draw his sword at any moment. "Is... everything alright up here, gentleman?" The owner questioned carefully.

William stepped forward from the door jamb, straightening his tunic, "Aye, just a misunderstanding it seems. I will pay for the repairs."

The owner nodded stiffly, gave them one last, long look, and retreated down the stairs, leaving them to their privacy.

Beddigan sighed, stepping back into his room, beckoning for William to join him. The Bear joined him shortly, carrying his bundle of clothing, boots, daggers, and sword with him.

Depositing his things on the little table near the window, William looked out over the dark streets, just as the sun started to peek over the horizon.

"Morning already." He commented, turning back to look at Beddigan who sat on the edge of the bed.

It had been a long few days since their initial meeting at the Wicked Mule Ale House. They had switched Inns every day, moving around the bustling city of San Vincent's Port, in hopes of creating a harder to follow trail; in the event that there were any assassins or hunters on their tail.

While collecting provisions for a journey to meet with Finnley, an old friend of Beddigan's, who may be able to help William with his problem, they had happened across a Wanted poster, requesting the return of a renegade solider Bear to the one and only Commander Rollstad; dead or alive. The price was a heavy one upon William's head and it hadn't taken long for the news to spread across the Lorring Sea.

Neither of them had slept well since they had made that discovery. They waited for a message from Finnley, confirming that they should make the trek up the coast to meet with him, but each day stretched longer and longer with no word.

It seemed equally dangerous and safe to stay in the city. On the one paw, it was large and busy, filled with people from all parts of the world, making it easier to blend in. But on the other paw, it was the main port contact for all of Katheyra.

Beddigan sighed again, "Maybe we should leave the city. I know we decided it was safer here but what about a small inland town? Word wouldn't have spread that far yet..." he trailed off.

William paced wearily, "It's possible," the Bear hedged, "or it could isolate us further and make us easier to target."

Beddigan made a frustrated sound in response. They had been back and forth with this argument since that first night. There really was no right answer; risks abound either way. So far, they had seen no real movement against them, though William had removed himself from public as much as possible, venturing out only at night and letting Beddigan gather information and supplies during the day.

Beddigan stood and dressed, "While it's still early, I say we go eat a real meal together and figure out what we should do. I know a quiet spot where they won't ask questions, and we can take alleys nearly the whole way there."

William nodded and went about dressing and affixing his weaponry.

Soon they were moving along the quiet cobblestone streets. Shutters were just starting to open, and few people were out and about. As soon as they were able, they slunk into an alley, darkened by the shade of the taller buildings, the low, early-morning sun unable to penetrate its depths.

They walked silently, with Beddigan in the lead. He stopped carefully each time the alley they were in intersected with a main road and subtly checked for signs of danger or pursuit before hurrying across into the alley on the other side. All the while, his mind raced, trying to come up with a solution for his dear friend, lest they could not successfully contact Finnley.

Moving swiftly across another intersection, he was part way down the alley before he realized he could no longer hear William's footfalls behind him. He whirled around and thrust his leather arm gauntlets in front of his face, just in time to block two daggers. They bit into the leather, one slicing clean through and digging into his flesh. The light grey fur of his arm darkened with blood.

Like a shadow, the lithe form leapt against the wall, and came down on him, sending them crashing to the hardpacked dirt of the alley, before he could even draw his sword. Struggling against the smaller body, wrapped almost entirely in dark cloth, Beddigan managed to shove away, rolling to his feet. His sword sliced the air with a flash, ready for the next attack, but his assailant just stood there, shaking softly. Beddigan then noticed the eyes — amber yellow and sparkling against the dark cloth of the mask.

Then he heard the soft, silky-smooth laughter of a voice he had not heard in ages.

"It appears you still have it, old man." The smoky, voice broke the silence, muffled only slightly by the cloth over her mouth.

Beddigan sheathed his sword, though he kept his paw at the ready near the hilt, "Shianne. What have you done with William?"

More laughter met him, "Annlose alive, Beddigan!" she giggled, "Have your senses really dulled that much?! You best pay more attention, lest a Wolf get you." Stepping aside, she allowed Beddigan a clear view down the alley and across the street into the previous alley, where he could make out William's large form slumped against the brick wall of a building.

Beddigan snarled, before stalking past her and across to the Bear, who upon closer inspection was only fast asleep, "What in the Warbler's name did you do to him?" he asked, knowing her to be right behind him despite not hearing even the slightest footfall. Shianne was known to most as Death's Whisper. A silent, deadly assassin, to be handled very carefully, or better yet avoided entirely.

When she didn't answer he turned to look at her. She had uncloaked her face, and Beddigan bit back a gasp at the sight of it.

"How?" he whispered, taking in the thick, dark gray fur of her face, which should have been the tell-tale red-gold of her people; the Foxes of Reene.

She grinned, eyes flashing mischievously, "There are many things to be found in the Ranier Islands to aid someone such as myself, dear Beddigan." William began to stir, and her eyes darted to him, "Including sleeping crystals."

Beddigan's brow furrowed, his mind filled with questions. As far as crystals were concerned, he had never heard of ones that could make a person do anything at all, let alone sleep. Crystals were used throughout the lands to affect the natural world. There were crystals to make fire and to cool or freeze. Crystals to create light or magnify. Crystals to create portals to move through the land quickly, though they were very rare and expensive. And every now and then a new crystal was discovered in the mines, but they always had to do with the natural world.

On top of that, many had set sail for the Ranier Islands, but none had every returned. Entire ships had disappeared in the mists surrounding the Islands, never to be seen again.

William yawned before shaking his head to clear it. He looked up at Beddigan and across at Shianne, "What in Annalose's name just happened?" he snarled, climbing to his feet.

Shianne laughed again, and Beddigan shot her a warning look, "Just an old friend with a new trick," he answered.

Shianne giggled, and stepped forward, pressing a paw against Beddigan's chest, "Oh we are more than old friends, aren't we Beddy?" Her voice twisted into a girlish caricature as she giggled, before she shoved him hard, sending him stumbling backward into William. They slammed back against the brick wall, and William stepped forward with a roar. Shianne whipped out her daggers with a feral smile, "Oh, now the fun part!" she cackled.

Beddigan leapt between his two friends, pushing them apart, "For Ardra's sake, can you two control yourselves for just one Warbler's Cursed moment?" he snarled. Turning to William he placed a paw on his friend's arm, feeling the muscles twitch beneath the thick, coarse fur, with barely restrained rage. "Step back, friend," he ordered softly. William shook as he stepped away from Shianne and moved a ways back down the alley.

Beddigan turned to Shianne who was using the sharp point of her dagger to pick her teeth, "If you've come for him, you'll have to go through me first."

Shianne tossed the dagger in the air, catching it effortlessly and stowing it inside her tunic. "A friend then. Well, that complicates things," she said, turning to gaze at William. "He is worth an awful lot. We could split it, and both still make out like Kings."

Beddigan crossed his arms across his chest, "Never." He said firmly.

Shianne made a frustrated sound, "I had heard that you had changed, but I should have known better," she growled.

Beddigan caught her wrist and pulled her back to look at him, "You should be very happy I haven't changed, because I know many who would give their right paw to get their paws on Death's Whisper."

Shianne's mouth curled into a snarl, which quickly broke into another silky laugh as she wrapped her arms around his neck, "Oh I missed you, Beddy!" she giggled.

Beddigan stiffened and didn't relax until she released him.

"Alright then. We'll make a trade then, yeah?" Beddigan didn't answer her. "Yes, yes, very good. I'll let your friend know." Shianne bounced off towards William.

Beddigan followed along stiffly. He caught William watching his face carefully as they approached.

"Everything okay?" the Bear asked. Beddigan forced a weak smile. Before he could answer, Shianne bounced off a wall and did a graceful pirouette in front of them.

"It's your lucky day, William! The most honorable Sir Beddigan T. Mouze has made me an offer of trade, so I will not be bagging and dragging you back to Mormant this day. In fact, I just may be your saving grace," she giggled again, batting her eyelashes at the Bear.

William just glared at her.

Beddigan let out a small grunt of annoyance, "Not Sir. Just Beddigan." He said flatly.

William waited for an explanation, but when Beddigan didn't offer one he turned to Shianne, "What's all this then? Who are you? And I'd like to see you try to bag and drag me without some dirty trick. You wouldn't stand a chance. Somebody better tell me what in this Warbler's Cursed world is going on."

Shianne whispered something into Beddigan's ear before leaping onto the uneven brick wall next to William's head, clinging inexplicably to the wall, "Not even you, my burly Bear friend, could evade Death's Whisper." And with that she scrambled and bounced off the walls of the alley onto the roof of a building and disappeared.

William watched until she was gone from sight before he turned to Beddigan, his mouth agape, "Death's Whisper? *The* Death's Whisper?" he asked softly.

Beddigan nodded, scrubbing his paws over his face. "An old friend," he said, weakly.

William stared at him. Beddigan let out a long, anguished sigh, walking down the alley, "Come. Let's have that meal and I'll explain it to you. It probably doesn't feel like it, but she's going to save your life."

***

"A life debt. Beddigan, I can't let you do that for me." William breathed out heavily, reeling from the story Beddigan had told over breakfast. A story of a little vixen kit from Reene, no more than seven turnings old, kept as a war prisoner in Fort Alline many years ago. Orphaned by the continuing war, she hadn't any family left when she was tossed into the cargo hold of the smelly, overcrowded ship and stolen from her homeland; in a village by the sea, just north of Reene's capital of Rilanda.

Her parents had been compliant with the Mormant authorities, but a rebellion had started up near their village and all were punished in the area for the loss of a few Mormant soldiers. Beddigan hadn't known how long she had lived in the disgusting work camp in Fort Alline when he first came across her, but from the look of her he knew she wouldn't last much longer.

On a rescue mission with Her Majesty's Royal Sapphire Brigade, to liberate several members of their own who had been captured and were set to be put to death, Beddigan had taken on the extra risk and successfully spirited Shianne away in the dark of night. He had taken her back to Illensdar and found a family to foster her, though she bonded with him strongly and would regularly turn up at the soldier barracks looking for him, and refusing to leave once she found him.

He would watch her, reading her stories, letting her rest knowing she was safe in his care, then he would take her home when he had a moment's peace, and the cycle would continue with her reappearing a few days later.

He had watched her grow and change until his life had taken a turn and he had fled across the land bridge to Katheyra. He hadn't even the time to say goodbye to her. He dared not even send a message, and so he had disappeared from her life along with everyone else's.

Several turnings later while on a break between adventures, he had come back to his room at an Inn after much ale, to find it occupied by a fully-grown Shianne. It was that night that she had informed him of the life debt she felt she owed him. She had joined an assassin's guild and had become a much harder woman than the sensitive kit he had rescued. From that night on they had seen each other every so often, and Beddigan had watched as she became more proficient as an assassin, and as her erratic behaviour increased.

"It is already done, friend." Beddigan said, taking a sip of tea, relishing the taste of honey blended with earl gray. "Besides, we don't have much in the way of options. This is the only way."

He watched his friend closely, seeing the pain of it all written across the Bear's face. To disappear, he would have to abandon his family. Ironic, considering taking care of them was what had gotten him into this mess in the first place. He would need to appear dead beyond a shadow of a doubt. For that, Death's Whisper was a perfect accomplice. After all, she didn't make a habit of leaving people alive.

Pushing back from the table, William pulled his cloak up to shadow his face. Beddigan dropped some gold coins on the table for their meal, nodded to the barmaid, and followed his friend out into the sunny street.

Even with William's cloak pulled up, they decided to take the alleys back as far as they could to their Inn. They needed to gather their supplies before night fell and then travel to the northern part of San Vincent's Port to the unfamiliar Inn Shianne had said she would meet them at.

It wasn't long before they were forced to leave the alleys and move onto the busy cobblestone streets as they neared the Inn they had been staying at. It was tucked away near the towering city wall with a bit of green space at its back.

Beddigan had been to this Inn many times before, so he knew the layout well. Two low stairs lead up to the big, swinging doors that lead to the entrance of the Inn. A flight of stairs to the left of the doorway lead up to the rooms, and a broad arch lead past the registration counter, into the common room where, no doubt, many patrons would be taking their fill of food and ale.

They slowed as they approached, noticing two Wolves loitering near the entrance. Though Katheyra was a bustling city, home to members of nearly all the species of the lands, Wolves were rarely seen outside of Mormant. Though they wore no uniforms, Beddigan was sure that they were soldiers from their stance and not-quite-concealed weaponry. He would recognize the Wolf-headed hilt of a Mormant soldier's sword anywhere. He veered down a side street quickly, with a knowing glance over his shoulder at William.

By the grim look on his friend's face, Beddigan knew that he had caught sight of the Wolves' weapons as well.

"I guess I won't be getting my extra cloak back." William muttered.

Beddigan groaned softly, thinking of all the supplies and rations left in his room. "I am not just leaving everything behind, William. Guards or no guards." Peering out around the corner he saw the Wolves were now questioning a couple of Badgers on their way into the Inn. "We just need to think of a plan. Maybe we could go in the back through the service entrance?"

William grunted, shaking his head, "No back entrance in this place, from what I've seen. Maybe we just walk up, take them if we have to?"

Beddigan scowled, first at the fact they had picked an Inn without a back entrance, and then at the idea of taking on two fully trained soldiers from Mormant. "They're military trained, so it would be a tough call on who would win. Plus, we don't need to attract any extra attention."

William nodded in agreement. They both fell silent, thinking about a way to get past the Wolves.

"Maybe just you go? They will be looking for me, or a pair, but not just any Mouse alone." William ventured, pacing back and forth across the narrow street.

Beddigan shook his head, "By now they could easily know we are together.

I'm surprised to see soldiers at all, even in disguise, and if they have made the connection..." He trailed off. Beddigan scrubbed his paws over his face in frustration and moved to peek around the corner again. He was surprised to see the entrance to the Inn bare now; no Wolves in sight.

He beckoned for William to look, scanning the area around the street and Inn for them, to no avail.

"Must have gone inside." William grumbled. "May have a shot if we go in and straight up the stairs. If they are in the common room they may not see us."

Beddigan nodded, stepping out into the street and signaling for William to wait. He walked out a few steps and looked around, making sure there wasn't an ambush waiting for them. When nothing happened and no one took any notice of him, he gestured for William to follow, and they moved swiftly to the Inn's entrance.

"Quickly. Keep your cloak up." Beddigan whispered, tugging his own up before moving into the Inn and directly up the stairs. As they moved down the hall, approaching his room, Beddigan kept his ears pricked for any sign of danger. The broken door to William's room still dangled on its hinges. Reaching for his doorknob he was pleased to find it still locked.

Hurryingly, he opened the door and ushered William in ahead of him. Closing the door and turning the lock, he blew out a relieved breath.

"About time you boys arrived," came the dusky tones of Shianne's voice. Beddigan whirled around to find her reclining on the bed. William was slumped against a table, snoring softly.

"What in this Warbler's Cursed world do you think you're doing?" Beddigan snarled.

Shianne rolled effortlessly to her feet and walked across the room to William, caressing his furry cheek, "Saving your life and your friend's life... and having a spot of fun." She answered with a giggle.

Beddigan shot her a pained look, "And putting him to sleep again is part of the fun, I take it?"

Shianne giggled, "Well, if you had a sleep crystal, wouldn't you want to use it?"

Beddigan stared at her, then shook his head, "Why aren't you waiting at the Two-Headed Horse like we planned?" he asked, changing the subject to get her back on track.

Shianne fiddled with a dagger, rolling it in her paws and tossing it lightly in the air, "Change of plans. Your friend here really did anger the wrong Wolf. There are more assassins than I anticipated as well as plenty of Mormant soldiers. They wear no uniforms, so I can't tell who commands them, but they are not here to play." She tucked her daggers away, pulling out a hard, wooden chair from the small table. Sitting, crossing her long legs and indicating for him to sit as well, she continued, "Our position was compromised, so I chose to meet you here. And I put your big friend here out so that we may discuss some sensitive information."

Beddigan sat and braced his head in his paws, "We needn't discuss that, Shianne. I know what was offered and I accept the consequences of that trade. We need to get William out of the city. And you need to hold up your end of the bargain." He could feel her eyes on him and when he looked up, he was surprised to see a glimmer of tears in them. She looked hurt.

"You think that I would deliver you to their paws? That I would put you where you found me and leave you there?" her voice quivered and Beddigan tried to hide his shock.

"I... I know what our bargain is. But... it's hard to know what to expect from you." He hedged.

A snarl curled Shianne's lip as she crossed her arms over her chest, "A life for a life. It's done. I owe you no longer, once William is free." Beddigan watched her as her eyes returned to their calm, deadened amber, all traces of tears disappearing, "That is the deal." Shianne stood quickly, the chair legs squealing briefly over the floor. "I will take care of the guard's downstairs. You wake the Bear and gather your things. It isn't going to be easy to get you out of the city, but I have a connection at the East Gate. Where will you go?"

Beddigan had been thinking of that since this plan first hatched, "We will go south to Windermere. It is the safest place I can think of."

Shianne nodded, "Meet me downstairs as soon as you have your things. We must move quickly if we are to get you out before nightfall."

Beddigan nodded as she slipped silently out of the room. He roused William who was infuriated at being put to sleep again. They gathered their things and moved carefully down the stairs to find Shianne waiting at the door to the Inn.

She smiled brilliantly at William, "Good day, sunshine! Did you have a nice nap?" she giggled.

Beddigan felt William tense next to him. Before he could say a word back to Shianne, Beddigan jumped in, "Now now, we haven't the time for games. Come, we must be quick. We have to get out of the city as soon as possible." William snarled softly but stayed his tongue and followed them outside, keeping his hood up around his face.

They moved quickly through the city, avoiding market squares and taking alleys as they could. The gates to the city were the least guarded and least busy between midday and evening so they arrived at the perfect time.

Along the way Shianne had disappeared ahead and returned, clearing the way of any potential soldiers or spies. They both were a bit awestruck by her proficiency.

As they approached the East Gate, Beddigan was pleased to see no Wolves in sight. Shianne approached the city guards who manned the gate, speaking softly to the Badger, and then quickly gestured for them to move to the front of the throng of people waiting to be processed and released.

Shoving a wad of parchment into Beddigan's paw, Shianne spoke quickly and quietly, "Go. I will watch to make sure you aren't tailed and then take care of my part of the bargain. You are on your own until you reach Toldsdale. Go to the Thirsty Mule Alehouse and ask for Garvin. Give him those papers and you will have access to a portal crystal." She grasped Beddigan's paw, "Be safe. Stay low. The debt is paid but you aren't without a friend in me, Beddigan." She leaned up and kissed his cheek.

Beddigan returned the kiss, stowed the parchment in his tunic, and turned away, moving with the rush of people outside of the city walls. William moved behind him as they picked their way through the crowd and headed towards the trail leading to Toldsdale.

Once they had gotten far enough away from the gate and the crowds had thinned, William grasped Beddigan's arm from behind, "Thank you, friend. I could never repay you for this."

Beddigan patted the Bear's shoulder, "What are friends for if not to help when needed? Come, we should be able to make it to Toldsdale by nightfall."

The two trudged on, the city wall of San Vincent's Port dwindling in the distance behind them.

***

"The Commander will see you now." A stiff Wolf clad in the royal red of Mormant's army lead Shianne through a door into a large, airy room in a very expensive Inn near San Vincent's Port's city center. A large Wolf, with silvery fur and piecing blue eyes, sat in a plain wooden chair. The only thing distinguishing this Wolf from the other Wolves in the room was a sash of black over his red doublet, with gold embossed lettering denoting his military rank of Commander.

"Death's Whisper... we meet at last." The Wolf growled softly, his eyes penetrating hers.

She dazzled a smile and bowed deeply, "The pleasure is mine, Commander Rollstad."

The Commander watched her closely for a moment, "You come to claim the price on William Bearhelm's head, then?" He questioned.

Shianne pulled an engraved dagger from her tunic and handed it to a soldier, who passed it to the Commander. It was engraved with the Bearhelm family crest and William's initials. He examined it closely, before handing it back to the soldier with a satisfied growl. "It is done. You may collect your fee on your way out." He said, gesturing dismissively to the doorway.

Shianne bowed again, turning on her heel to leave. She stopped just short of the doorway and turned back to face him, "I did come across some very sensitive information in my hunt for the Bear, Commander. Some information I am sure would be of great interest to you..." The Commander eyed her expectantly, "For a price." She added with a feral grin.

Commander Rollstad waved dismissively again, "I don't barter for information with spies. Be gone."

Shianne bowed again hastily and turned. "Thank you for your time, Commander. Perhaps I will see you again soon in Mormant, as I am sure someone in the military will care what I know about a certain Mouse." She said as she flounced away.

Chapter 3: They Call Him Captain Linley

Beddigan was thrown up hard against the wall of the small, deeply below-deck cabin that he had been living in for nearly a week. He was aboard the Fillsner's Muse, a trade and passenger ship running from San Vincent's Port to the little coastal town of Rannan's Point, on the northeast coast of Sinerrah's largest island. The island was home to the country's capital city, Orreka, which was just southwest of William's home Village of Doucent.

Several weeks had passed since he and William had fled San Vincent's Port, and news of William's apparent death at the paws of Death's Whisper had spread across the land like wildfire. They had used the portal crystal that Shianne had procured for them to get from Toldsdale to Windermere in a single step and had laid low and disappeared into the small town. Lucky for them, the townspeople were more than happy to assist Beddigan and his friend after he had saved them from the Dragon, Galantus.

They had been staying in an empty house, still furnished by its previous owner, who had perished during one of the Dragon's rampages. They had taken their meals by delivery from The Three-Headed Rabbit Inn, feasting on thick stews and crusty bread rolls, finally getting a much-needed break while they stayed under cover.

It didn't take long for the town elders to come knocking, to tell them that they had indeed received word of William's death, confirmed by the Mormant Military Commander Rollstad, through Katheyra's Council of Elders. Once the news was received, relief and then sorrow settled in for William, as he had now effectively abandoned his former life. He could no longer wear the Bearhelm family crest. He could never go home to Sinnerah and see his wife and children again. He could no longer be anything more than William; a Bear, an adventurer. Alone.

William had warned his wife and children before leaving Sinerrah in search of Beddigan that he may never return, though he had hoped there would be a way to avoid that. He still hoped that it would one day be possible for him to return home, though that seemed to be a hope for a very distant future.

In the meantime, Beddigan was to deliver all of the carefully removed pieces of Bearhelm crested jewelry, clothing and weaponry, along with as much coin as William had left, to his grieving widow. This is the task that had brought him to the ship sailing across the Lorring Sea.

Beddigan steadied himself as the ship rocked beneath his feet, feeling the meal of spicy vegetable pie turning to rock in his stomach. He had never liked sea travel. He liked it even less at this very moment. He slid open the sliding door to his tiny cabin and moved out of the ship's belly and up the several flights of stairs to the deck.

According to his calculations they should be arriving in

Rannon's Point sometime that day. A burst of fresh salt air tickled his whiskers as he strode across the bustling deck. Sailors called orders to one another, the captain's voice chief among them. He peered down at the churning azure water and then turned, looking towards the back of the ship where the great wheel sat, past the billowing white sails. Standing on a crate as so to reach, wearing a large black hat with a bright red feather in it, was the captain of this great ship; small in stature but big in heart.

Captain Linley was the single greatest Badger to sail the Lorring Sea. He was very petite, even for a Badger, though he had reportedly never lost a ship to pirates and had never run aground in one of his ships. There were even tales of him sailing beyond the mapped areas of the Trelill Sea, though his grin dropped away if you asked him about it. His squawking voice rose above the others as he called out orders to his shipmates.

"Land Ho!" called the Badger from the crow's nest, and Beddigan turned to look ahead. There on the horizon was the lush green expanse of the islands of Sinerrah. They were very large; huge land masses stretching out for great distances. Coming down from the north the full scope of their immensity was easy to see.

Also, a benefit to coming in from the north, was the ability to see in the distance, on the eastern side of the great island, the huge, Bear-made bridge that connected the capital island to the middle one. A feat of engineering that was not seen outside of Sinerrah, the Bears had created something no other country could match: a bridge to connect land masses. The first time Beddigan had caught sight of it he was astounded by its grandeur. The first time he had walked across it he was stricken by not only the enormity of the task of building such a structure, but the brilliance behind its design.

The Bears were often written off as fighters and hunters, with little written history or creative works stemming from their people, but the bridges alone proved otherwise.

Beddigan breathed a final sigh of relief at the sight of Sinerrah on the horizon and headed back down below deck to collect his things.

**

Having disembarked the ship and arranged for a carriage, Beddigan let himself fall asleep on the long ride from Rannan's Point to the village of Doucent. He slept soundly on the wide bench seat, with its soft pillows and flannel blankets. The driver shook him awake once they had reached their destination, and Beddigan tipped him handsomely for the quick and quiet ride.

He moved through the village, past the main shopping square and headed east as William had advised him. He walked down the path through the woods, the lush trees bathing him in dappled sunlight. Soon, he came to the discreet stone marker at the mouth of an adjoining path, that held the Bearhelm crest.

Winding through the trees, the path opened into a clearing and Beddigan spotted a tidy white stone house with a bright red roof. In the distance, past the house, he saw two Bear cubs running around, and a female Bear knelt over a garden patch.

As he neared the female Bear he cleared his throat, hoping to avoid startling her. The woman turned around with a growl, brandishing her hoe like a weapon, and Beddigan jumped back as she swung wildly at him.

"Woah, woah! Elenya! Hold on! I am not here to hurt you!" Beddigan yelped, jumping back again as she took another swing.

Still brandishing the hoe, the Bear narrowed her eyes, "What other reason would you have to be here?" she said in a low growl.

He met her eyes and said, "I am a friend..." With news of William's passing still so fresh it felt best to keep it secret and safe while out in the open, despite the feeling of privacy that the homestead gave them.

After a moment, the Bear's eyes flew open wide in recognition.

Beddigan noticed the two cubs had approached and were huddled by the house, peering around the corner.

"If we could go inside, Ma'am, I have some things to share with you."

Elenya nodded, and Beddigan followed her to the oak door. She stopped for a moment, hesitating before opening the door, then called out, "Elisha! Aeron! Here. Now." The two cubs Beddigan had seen playing in the meadow came slinking around the corner of the house. Elenya waited for them to be right near her before she spoke again, "Go inside and get Erikkson. He could use some fresh air. Go to the stream for a bit. And no sneaking back to eavesdrop. I've raised you better than that." The cubs nodded and pushed past their mother into the house.

Beddigan and Elenya waited in silence a few moments before they returned, each holding onto the arm of another cub, whose brown fur was thin and lacked the rich colouring of his brother and sister. The cub's eyes were yellowed and bloodshot, and his frame much thinner. Beddigan's heart thudded heavily at the sight of such a young Bear so obviously ill, and began to understand why William had been driven to do what he had done.

Once the cubs were out of earshot Elenya moved into the house, beckoning him to follow. She gestured to a hard-backed wooden chair near a round, beautifully carved oak table.

Beddigan took a seat and waited as Elenya moved around the small, combined living, kitchen, and dining room. She retrieved a metal teapot from a shelf above the basin sink and filled it with water from a ladle and bucket by the door. Placing it on the counter she dunked a clear crystal with a bright red center attached to a long chain into the pot and waited a few moments until steam rose from it. Placing the crystal aside she added herbs from jars to a little fabric sachet and dropped them into the pot. She carried it to the table, setting it on a woven mat and retrieved two heavy crockery mugs from another shelf, before taking the seat opposite Beddigan.

"So, you must be that infamous Mouse then. I have heard much of you, Beddigan. What can you tell me of my husband?" she said, her voice flat.

Beddigan felt his mouth dry up under the hard gaze of the Bear across the table. He cleared his throat and rustled with his pack, taking the cloth-wrapped bundle of William's possessions out and placing it on the table, sliding it across to Elenya.

"He is gone, but not in the way you have likely heard, Ma'am. He wished for you to have these for the cubs as they grow up." He dug through his bag again and lifted a heavy coin purse out, sliding it across to her as she unwrapped the bundle and surveyed the contents. "And this as well," he added.

The silence stretched out as she carefully looking over the contents and then packed them up again, pushing them aside with the coins.

"Well, that's that then." she said coldly, before standing to pour tea. She shoved one of the mugs across the table to him, steaming fragrant liquid spilling over the rim, before she gathered the belongings and coins and disappeared into one of the two other rooms the house held.

Beddigan sniffed the steaming beverage and grinned. Good Sinerrahan tea was often hard to find outside the country. He took a moment and savored it in silence.

Elenya broke the silence as she entered the room again. She opened her mouth to speak and then froze. Beddigan turned, following her eye line through one of the un-shuttered windows, across the meadow to the path he had just walked up, minutes before. Two soldiers in full Mormant military regalia were just entering the clearing.

Beddigan stood quickly, jostling the table and nearly spilling the contents of the mugs, "Get the children and hide!" he told Elenya, moving to approach the door, paw on the hilt of his sword.

The Bear stopped him before he reached it though with a large paw on his chest, "Do not presume to rescue me, *Beddigan T. Mouze*," she hissed. "I am not one to be bullied in my own home. Stay here and be quiet," she snarled, pushing him away from the door and letting it slam behind her.

Beddigan frowned, but obeyed, and crouched near the window where he could watch and listen, and help should the need to arise.

Elenya stood near the front of the house, watching the Wolves approach. When they were in earshot, she called out, "What brings two of Mormant's finest to my doorstep?" Beddigan nearly laughed out loud at the sneer in her voice.

The Wolves stopped in front of her, "We bring sad news to the widow Bearhelm, as William has died in the field. Are you the Elenya Bearhelm we seek?"

Elenya's eyes widened, "I have heard. Thank you for coming all this way but it is an unsurprising piece of news after I heard you lot were hunting him down. Hardly in the field," she snarled at them.

The Wolf who had first spoken frowned, "As a member of our militia he wrote his own fate by betraying us. It is entirely his fault he sits in the ground now. Were he as courageous and honorable as a Wolf, he would never have ended up like this."

The other Wolf nodded along, "You should be kinder to your betters. You are all alone out here now. You shouldn't forget that," the Wolf snarled. "It can be very dangerous for a mother all alone in the woods…"

Beddigan's grip tightened on his sword hilt as fury bloomed anew in his chest. He watched as Elenya crossed her arms across her chest, her face a mask of rage as well. "Is that a threat, Wolf?" she growled.

The second Wolf stepped forward and grabbed her by the shoulder. Before the Wolf could speak or Beddigan could rise to burst out of the house, there was a flash of silver and fur as Elenya buried two wickedly long daggers into the soldier: one into his stomach, and the other into his neck. With a wicked growl, Elenya threw the bleeding and gasping Wolf to the ground.

The other soldier stared, mouth agape, as Elenya leapt at him before he could even draw his sword.

Beddigan burst outside then, only to find he wasn't needed at all. Elenya rose from the still body of the Wolf, muzzle dripping telltale red and eyes ablaze. She stalked towards Beddigan and the other Wolf, who was still conscious but shallow of breath. Beddigan stepped aside as Elenya knelt next to the Wolf, removing her daggers.

He gasped for air, "They'll have your life for this..." he spat out.

Elenya grinned, a fearsome sight with the blood of the other Wolf still bright on her teeth, "Sinerrah law allows for self-defense to the point of death when threatened. I thought my *betters* would know that." She slammed her paw down and the Wolf went still and quiet. She stood, and turned to Beddigan, watching his face for any sign of danger.

Beddigan struggled to keep his face calm amidst the carnage, "Clearly you were right, ma'am. I needn't worry about you."

She stared at him for a moment and then nodded stiffly, "Leave. Now."

Beddigan settled his pack on his shoulders and hurried past her up the path, stepping gingerly around the blood soaking into the grass and dirt. As he reached the road back to Doucent, his mind replayed and reeled over what had just happened. He was now certain, more than ever, that the Bears were not to be trifled with.

Chapter 4: Water, Water, Everywhere...

Upon returning to San Vincent's Port after his brief visit to Sinerrah, Beddigan had planned to hole up in his favourite Inn for a couple of days, having not gotten much rest on the lengthy voyage home across the Lorring Sea. He had figured he would have plenty of time to take a few days' rest before taking on adventures that would take him south, towards his temporary home of Windermere, and reunite him with William.

Captain Linley had tried to persuade him to stay aboard as a temporary part of the crew, as they had some dangerous cargo to transport, but Beddigan had bowed out of the offer, desperately seeking to get back on land. He had spent the majority of the trip home hung over the side of the ship, trying to ease his upset stomach. If he didn't see another boat for a turning... it would still be too soon.

He had barely reached his choice of Inn, The Swishing Serpent, near the northern gate of the city, before he was approached by a young, willowy Badger sow. He hadn't even had time to sip the ale that sat freshly poured upon his little corner table in the bustling common room. She had anxiously explained that she was from a seaside village just north of the city, and that she was desperate for his help. Fishermen had been disappearing at an alarming rate, and recently her father and brother had been lost. No bodies had washed ashore and the boats and canoes they had been on had never been seen again.

The village had little to offer Beddigan in terms of payment, but he knew he couldn't leave this poor young Badger with no family and no answers. And to be honest, the mystery of it all had piqued his interest. He had spent the rest of that night at the Inn, and they had departed the following morning by carriage.

During the ride to the village of Marcine Bay, Beddigan learned that the Badger's name was Ashryn, and that her mother had died when she was young. She was of marrying age but the village she lived in was quite small and informal, so she had yet to take a suitor. With all the disappearances in the past turning, marriage was the last thing on her, and the other villagers', minds.

"If people have been going missing as long as a turning, why did your father and brother go out fishing? That seems a bit foolish." Beddigan asked as the carriage bumped along the worn dirt track up the coast.

Ashryn frowned, "It's our livelihood. We haven't much else in Marcine Bay except fish. Fish Market for trade, fish restaurants for food. Fish. We are a fishing people, or did I not make that clear?" she said crossly.

Beddigan held up his paws apologetically, "I apologize. It was not meant as an insult. How come you didn't seek out someone to help before now?"

Ashryn sighed, "We did, but once he got to our village, he demanded a portion of his fee up front. We haven't much money and little experience with Adventurers, so our mayor paid it to him... and he fled that night."

Beddigan's lip curled in a snarl, "Coward."

The carriage abruptly came to a stop. Beddigan peered out the window at the little buildings clustered together at the top of a high bluff. He could smell the salt air and hear the waves crashing down below. The coast grew rockier and craggier from San Vincent's Port as it flowed northward, until becoming one with the Snowcap Mountains.

The village of Marcine Bay sat high above a narrow strip of rocky beach. Steps carved into the side of the cliff helped to bridge the well-worn pathways down the steep incline. A boardwalk with several wooden docks jutted out into the gently lapping sea, which was partially sheltered by the concavity of the cliffs.

Once out of the carriage, Ashryn lead him into town, towards its only Inn, The Mariner's Boots, where the town Elders would be gathered.

Just as they arrived, the door burst open and a wild eyed, young male Badger burst out into the street. Ashryn yelped and caught the Badger as they toppled to the ground. Beddigan growled and hauled the Badger off of the sow by the back of his tunic.

Once she stood and got a look at the newcomer, Ashryn shoved Beddigan aside, throwing herself into the Badger's arms, "Aliott!" she sobbed, nearly strangling the newcomer in her grip. After a moment of hugging and sobbing, Ashryn finally let go of the other Badger, turning to Beddigan, "Beddigan, this is my brother, Aliott. Alliott, this is Beddigan T. Mouze. He's here to help us!"

Beddigan nodded to him, eyeing the Badger curiously, "Didn't you say your brother went down with your father's fishing boat?"

Aliott spoke up, "That I did, Sir. Woke up washed ashore up the coast a ways. Lucky I didn't break my back on them rocks."

Ashryn gripped Aliott's forearm, "Father? What happened? Did you see anyone else?"

Aliott shook his head sadly, visibly struggling with his words, "There... it was huge! I don't know how I got away." The Badger stammered and gasped, dissolving into a coughing fit.

Beddigan handed Aliott his water canteen, speaking quietly, "Perhaps we should go inside and sit a moment, and then you can fill us all in." Both Badgers nodded and they made their way inside the Inn.

Having taken seats at a long table with several other older Badgers seated at it, notably the villages council of Elders and the other families that had lost loved ones, Ashryn asked her brother to explain what had happened.

"We were sailing out past the North Point, cuz we'd heard there was a spot of great fishing there and our count has been low this month. All a sudden things got foggy. I swear it had blown in from no wheres! We tried to turn back but the wind died all together. I took the oars while father secured everything in case of storm and then suddenly the boat was hit hard by something. All I remember's after that was a flash of green. A burst of red... and scales. And teeth. A long tail. A sea serpent like from the stories! Then I woke up, up shore a bit. Took me this long to get back with the cliffs as they are up there." He took a long drink of his ale, "T'wasn't an easy route home."

Everyone at the table had eyes on Alliot, awestruck by the tale. Everyone except Beddigan, that is.

"Tell me, Aliott, were there any other fishermen in the area when the fog rolled in. Did you see any boats or canoes at all?" Beddigan questioned.

Aliott thought for a moment, "No, come to think of it. We saw a couple fellows in the bay headed south as we headed north but that's it."

Beddigan's brow furrowed deeper, "But surely if you had heard of this great fishing spot others would have headed that way as well, to take advantage of it?" he posed the question to the table. Other Badgers began to murmur.

Beddigan caught a flash of anger cross Aliott's face before it was replaced completely to a mask of sorrow, "Not too many of us left," he answered flatly.

Beddigan glanced at Ashryn, who was staring at her brother intently, "He's right. Plenty of the villagers won't take the risk very often anymore," she said.

Beddigan gladly accepted a bowl of steaming soup and a plate of crusty bread from a serving maid who made her way around the table depositing food in front of people. He could feel everyone at the table's eyes on him as he swirled his bread in the white broth of the soup and took a bite, chewing thoughtfully.

"Well," he said after swallowing, "There is only one way to get to the bottom of this." He took a few more bites of the meal, knowing everyone was watching him expectantly.

Finally, Aliott made a strangled sound, "What? What is the way?"

Beddigan set his spoon down and scanned the group at the

table, his eyes settling on Aliott. "I'm going to need a boat."

***

"You can't be serious!" Ashryn gasped, hurrying to keep up with Beddigan as he made his way down the steep paths and stairs to the boardwalk below the village. After he had made it clear he was going to need to see this alleged serpent up close, the table had erupted with a combination of fear, worry, and dread.

Many were worried that Beddigan would disappear like the rest, without a trace, leaving them with no one to help them. Some feared he would somehow draw the beast back to the village and they would be wiped out completely. Aliott had left abruptly to secure him a boat and was now waiting on the boardwalk for him.

"How else do you propose to resolve this mystery, Ashryn?" Beddigan asked as they stepped off the final stair and onto the wooden walkway.

Ashryn huffed, "Well, I don't know but I don't want to be responsible for your death!"

They approached Alliot who stood at the mouth of one of the docks, a small rowboat bobbing in the waves just behind him.

"I have no intention of dying, Ashryn." Beddigan said, raising a paw in greeting to Aliott as they came to a stop in front of him.

Ashryn huffed again, "You can't do this alone! Have you ever even *been* on a rowboat? This is madness!" she threw her paws up in the air in frustration.

Beddigan chuckled, reaching up and pulling her paws down,

tucking her arms back down at her sides. "Ashryn, calm down. I have bested far worse than a sea serpent. I came to help and help I shall." Ashryn's brow furrowed, but she nodded silently anyways.

"He won't be alone, Ash," Aliott interjected, "I'm going with him."

Beddigan spun around to look at Aliott, "Is that really wise? You are the only survivor. Were something to happen to me..." he trailed off, acutely aware of Ashryn now sobbing softly behind him.

Aliott stepped around him and embraced his sister, "Ash, he needs a guide to have a hope at all. And someone who has their sea legs. I came back once, and I'll do it again, you can bet on that! I won't leave you alone," he tried to comfort his sister.

Beddigan noticed that Aliott ignored his question but kept quiet. Once the siblings had separated, Beddigan smiled at Aliott, "Thank you, Alliot. No one else offered and I do need a guide and some help with the boat. Your courage knows no bounds."

Aliott nodded, kissed his sister's cheek one last time and climbed into the boat, readying it for departure. Beddigan placed his paws on each of Ashryn's shoulders, "I'll watch over him. Chin up, girl," he smiled at her, before climbing into the boat.

The next bit was a flurry of activity as Aliott barked orders at him and they gradually moved away from the dock, out into the bay. Beddigan could see the townspeople lined up along the bluffs edge, and Ashryn still standing on the boardwalk as they headed out into the sea, further from the shore.

Soon they were well on their way, passing the North Point of the bay.

Beddigan watched the horizon, both to still his wobbly stomach and for any sign of other ships or the mysterious fog from Aliott's tale.

"We're just about to the place where —" Aliott's voice abruptly cut off as the wind huffed and fog manifested around them, rushing to encapsulate the boat.

Beddigan leapt up, nearly toppling over the edge of the boat, paw on his sword hilt. He whirled around trying to gather his bearings in the dense fog when suddenly a *thunk* and sharp blast of pain exploded in his shoulder. Looking down, bewildered he saw the plain, dull hilt of a dagger sticking out of his shoulder just above the joint.

"Son of a Warbler!" he hissed. "Aliott! Are you okay?" he called, ducking down to hopefully avoid any other daggers that may come flying at him.

The fog was so thick, he couldn't see the other end of the boat where Aliott had been standing. Then came another *thunk*, and an explosion of pain this time in his thigh, just above the knee. Another dull-hilted dagger.

"Aliott!" he whispered urgently, creeping forward, swallowing a groan of pain. The shadow of Aliott was suddenly visible through the fog. Beddigan looked up as the mist thinned to see the Badger grinning down at him. Aliott hefted one of the heavy wooden oars.

"Father always said the worst part about Adventurers is that they can't never mind their own business." The oar crashed down and Beddigan slumped against the side of the boat.

***

Beddigan startled awake, blinking against the dim light filtering into the room from a slit beneath the door. His head was pounding. He found his paws tied behind his back, when he instinctively tried to raise a paw to what he was sure was a large, throbbing bump on the back of his head. Slowly, the whole ordeal on the boat with Aliott came drifting back.

The daggers had been removed from his shoulder and leg, and the wounds had been bandaged while he had been unconscious. He felt the familiar roll of the sea and realized he was once again in the belly of a ship. *I've had enough sea travel for a lifetime*, he thought, turning his wrists against the scratchy rope that bound them, searching for a weakness in the knots.

He struggled to get to his feet, his entire body aching from being slumped in the tiny, windowless storage room. His sword and dagger were both missing, along with his coin purse and crystals pouch. The room was empty except for a burlap sack of oranges, with more than a few reeking of rot, leaving him little to free himself with.

He heard several sets of heavy footfalls beyond the door and the murmuring of conversation. With a bark of chuckling laughter, the door flew open and light streamed into the room. Beddigan blinked hard as his eyes adjusted, until Aliott's face came into clear view.

The Badger was grinning at him in a most irksome manner. "Well, you're awake then. *Finally!*" Aliott chuckled. A couple of other Badgers that Beddigan couldn't recall having ever seen before, flanked his foe and chuckled alongside him.

"Apologies for the inconvenience of a late sleep, though if memory serves, you had a paw in putting me out," Beddigan drawled sarcastically.

Aliott's grin turned into a frown, "Not just a paw, I put you out cold all myself! The great Beddigan T. Mouze, outwitted by a simple fisherman's son." His cohorts cheered and patted Aliott on the back.

Beddigan waited for them to quiet, "I highly doubt any of this was your idea, but children do like to play dress up, so go ahead, tell me more about how you bested me."

Aliott's face twisted in anger and his paw shot out, clocking Beddigan in the face, adding to his already pounding headache. He slumped against the wall a moment, the room spinning. Paws gripped his forearms, hauling him out of the little room and through the innards of the ship. Aliott stalked ahead of them. They stopped at the foot of the stairs leading up to the ship's deck.

"I'll take him from here boys," Aliott ordered as he turned to face Beddigan. The other men drifted away. "Turn around," he ordered.

Beddigan turned slowly, so that his back was to Aliott. He heard the telltale scrape of a dagger sliding from its sheath. A moment of fear was followed swiftly by the tug and scrape of the dagger against the bonds holding his wrists together, and Beddigan breathed a sigh of relief. Once his wrists were free, he rubbed them softly, his fur tinged a deep read where they had chafed the skin beneath his fur.

He turned back to face Aliott, "Why take me captive just to free me?"

Aliott tossed the bloody bonds aside and sheathed his dagger with a feral grin, "You are not free. You will never be free again. But we hardly need an unarmed Mouse in bonds, according to

Captain Marlog anyways. I'd have left you trussed up at least a bit longer."

Beddigan's frown deepened as Aliott led him up the stairs and onto the busy ship's deck.

The ship bobbed and rolled in the waves and Beddigan could see only more sea on the horizon, not a speck of land in sight. As Aliott led him towards the back of the ship, Beddigan surveyed the crew, looking for any familiar or pleasant faces for the escape he knew he would need to attempt. Unfortunately, few met his eyes at all and those that did smiled cruelly with glowering eyes.

Aliott drug Beddigan up a couple of stairs and tossed him roughly onto the deck, "As you requested, Captain. The Mouse."

Beddigan winced as two large paws gripped his injured arm and yanked him to his feet. He stifled a groan of pain, swallowing it down. He found himself standing before a tall, lean Wolf, dressed in tan breeches, a long navy doublet, and a white collared shirt. Gleaming black boots and a broad black hat with a white feather completed the ensemble. *Pirates*, Beddigan thought with a grimace.

The Wolf's teeth gleamed as he looked down over him, "Not just a Mouse, dear boy, a *very* famous Mouse, indeed!" Beddigan held his expression carefully neutral. It was very rare to see a Wolf outside of Mormant that was not a soldier. "Though from your meager possessions, you must keep your wealth locked up somewhere."

Beddigan didn't answer.

Aliott spoke, "According to my sister, he is pretty near the top Adventurer in all Katheyra. No family to speak of. Should have quite a pretty fortune built up somewheres."

Captain Marlog's smile turned a bit sharper as he turned to

Aliott, "Do not presume to educate me, *boy*. I know more that you will ever know about *Sir* Beddigan."

Beddigan's shoulders sunk down at the sound of his former title. He had hoped that Captain Marlog was only in it for his coin, and didn't know about his past, and about how much he was worth to Mormant, or his home country of Illensdar. For all he knew they were sailing towards Mormant right now. His eyes lingered on a dagger hanging from Aliott's belt. "Just Beddigan..." he muttered.

The Wolf barked out laughter, "It speaks!" The laughter continued on as Beddigan started to formulate a hasty plan to get the dagger from Aliott. Captain Marlog interrupted his thoughts, "You Mice always have to stick your noses in where they don't belong. Though I don't blame you for following that pretty little Badger back to Marcine Bay." Beddigan heard Alliot's laughter cease abruptly.

"For someone who seems to know so much about me," Beddigan said, directing his full attention at the Captain, "I am surprised you had your boy here unbind me. You should know I have no need of weapons."

Marlog chuckled at him, "You definitely have the arrogance that precedes you, but you have no chance of escape."

Beddigan chuckled back, "I have escaped far worse."

Captain Marlog nodded slowly, his laughter fading, "Aye, this you have. This is something that we share, dear Mouse. Though I have a feeling you underestimate me."

Beddigan dodged to the left, covering a grimace of pain and snatched the dagger from Aliott's belt sheath, twisting the young Badger around and holding the point of the dagger to his neck, "Perhaps you are the one underestimating things,

Captain."

With a swish of his doublet, Captain Marlog fished out a pouch and plucked a crystal from it. Beddigan's eyes widened as he saw the crystal glint in the sunlight, the colour of hot blue flame. Mist formed instantly and started to thicken the air round the ship. The ship rocked harder as the sea churned around them.

With a roar and a font of sea water, a giant beast, a Kraken split the surface, its tentacles reaching up high over the ship's mast. The dagger Beddigan had been holding clattered to the ship's deck, as Aliott quickly broke his hold, moving out of reach.

Captain Marlog turned to look at Beddigan, with the Kraken framed dramatically behind him, looking shadowy and dark in the growing mist, "I think not, Beddigan. I think not."

***

Beddigan sat in a plush chair across from Captain Marlog, a wide desk littered with papers and maps between them. His head was still spinning from the encounter with the Kraken, a beast which he had never seen before, aside from story books. And even in those stories, he had never heard of a Kraken that could be controlled by anyone.

Another mysterious crystal, like the one Shianne had used to put William to sleep. *Likely from the Ranier Islands*, Beddigan thought. *How are people getting there?* he wondered, tucking that question away in the back of his mind for further thought later.

After a few scribbles on a map, Captain Marlog returned his quill pen to the fountain and looked across the desk at Beddigan, reclining back in his seat. They were alone in the Captain's quarters, the rest of the crew out sailing the ship. He had overheard they were headed to a rendezvous point but had been too distracted to catch exactly where that would be.

"I know your fear, Beddigan. It is written all over your face," Captain Marlog said.

Beddigan frowned in response, "I haven't had the best of experiences on the business end of an armed Wolf," he retorted.

Marlog laughed, "That isn't the fear. You know you are worth more to me healthy than damaged or dead."

Beddigan looked at his wounds pointedly in response, "So, these stab wounds were necessary then?" he questioned; voice laced with sarcasm.

Marlog frowned, "No, that Aliott is a bit of a wild card. A bit unhinged, really." Beddigan sat in silence. "Regardless, the fear is much larger than wounds. I know that fear. The fear of being gift-wrapped and sent to Strille, to face your tormentors. To lose your war."

Beddigan caught a curiously sad glint in the Captain's eyes, "What would you know of it, Wolf? I know Mormant frowns upon defectors, but a Wolf's blood still runs pure, does it not?"

The Captain pushed back from his desk, getting up to stretch and pace, peering out the windows of the cabin. "Let's just say you and I have more in common than you think. I would be no more welcome in Strille than you."

Beddigan was shocked but retained his composure, "So... what have you been doing with these disappearing fishermen? This has been going on far too long for you to simply be trying to bait me?"

The Captain plunked back into his chair, propping his legs up on the desk. "There is money in selling ships to Mormant. And slaves. And with the Kraken, it is fast and easy to move the product across the Lorring Sea."

Beddigan frowned again, "But I thought you just said Mormant had no love for you?"

Captain Marlog smiled ferally, "They know better than to mess with a Kraken."

Beddigan couldn't help but smile, "Fair enough. So, what am I here for then? If you aren't going to turn me in to Mormant, what purpose do I have for you?"

Captain Marlog grinned for a moment and then let the grin fade away, "Originally, I just needed you out of the way, so as to keep this endeavor going. Then, when Aliott brought you in and let me know your name, I was planning to let you off with your life in exchange for the vast majority of your fortune. But now, dear Beddigan, I have grown quite fond of you. I suggest we make a deal."

Beddigan's eyes shot up in shock, "A deal? What kind of deal?"

Captain Marlog sprung up from his chair and moved around the desk, resting his paws upon Beddigan's shoulders. "I let you go, with all the belongings you came aboard with, and you don't tell a soul about this ship, her Captain, or the crystals he carries. And should we cross paths again, you owe me a favour."

Beddigan stared, feeling the weight of the Wolf's paws on his shoulders, thinking over the words Marlog had just said, "An enticing offer, Captain Marlog, but I do have one condition."

Marlog walked around the desk again, retaking his seat. He eyed Beddigan under steepled claws, "Speak it then."

Beddigan stood now, grimacing in pain from his wounded leg, "You leave Marcine Bay alone and trouble the fishermen from there no more. I won't pursue anything else I hear of lost fisherman along Katheyra's coast, provided you leave Marcine Bay alone."

Captain Marlog frowned a moment, stroking his chin while he thought over Beddigan's counteroffer. He stretched his paw across the desk with a flash of his teeth in a grin, "Deal." Beddigan reached across and shook, ignoring the pain in his wrists.

Captain Marlog led him out of the cabin and back on to the sunny deck of the ship, calling out, "Alliot! Here boy, now."

Alliot came loping towards them, "Aye Captain, shall I bind and toss the Mouse back in his hole?" the Badger questioned with a sneering look at Beddigan.

Morlag shook his head, "Fetch his gear and ready one of the rowboats. Beddigan will be leaving us."

Aliott gaped at his Captain, "Leave us? You're just letting him go?" he yelped.

Marlog reached forward, grabbing a pawful of the Badger's tunic, hauling him up close, "Was that you just *questioning* my orders, welp?"

Aliott shook his head hastily, "No. No, no, sorry Sir. I misspoke!" he begged.

The Captain tossed him down onto the deck, snarling, "Do as I say then."

Aliott scrambled to his feet, "This way, *Sir Beddigan*," he said with a hint of a sneer.

Beddigan followed the young Badger as he disappeared below decks. He hadn't time to let his eyes adjust before he reached the bottom of the stairs but caught the flash of silver as a sword swung towards his face. He quickly ducked and rolled out of the way, the sword sinking into the wooden handrail of the stairs.

Aliott snarled and threw a dagger, while trying to yank the sword free of the handrails grip. Beddigan dodged the dagger easily, just as Aliott wrenched his sword loose.

Beddigan was backed into a corner and the young Badger was advancing, "The Captain is a fool to let you go. He will thank me for this." Just before Aliott could swing his sword at Beddigan, the Badger's eyes grew wide and his body stiffened. He fell forward, sword clattering to the ground, and Beddigan saw Marlog standing just behind him. Blood darkened the Badger's tunic where the hilt of a long dagger still jutted out.

"Foolish boy," the Captain muttered before turning away. Two other Badgers of the crew drug the body away and another retrieved his belongings.

Beddigan sighed as he strapped his sword and pouches back onto his belt, claws digging into his coin pouch absentmindedly.

That evening, after a long row on a small boat, Beddigan finally reached the boardwalk of Marcine Bay. It was nearly nightfall, and just a single lantern blew in the wind as he tied the little boat up and started the grueling climb to the village above.

Once up top the cliffs, he walked slowly, exhausted from the journey, towards the Inn. The door burst open as he approached and Ashryn flew through the night towards him.

"Beddigan! You're alive!" she squealed. It occurred to him that he had no idea how long he had been gone. Ashryn flung her arms around him. Badgers were trailing out of the Inn to cluster around them in the street. Ashryn drew back, her eyes brimming with tears, "What of Aliott?" she asked.

Beddigan placed a paw on her shoulder, "I'm sorry Ashryn. He was lost in a battle. But he fought valiantly. You should be very proud." His gut tightened at such a lie, but he knew there was no harm in it.

Ashryn nodded, tears trickling down her cheeks. Beddigan pulled her into his arms again and let her sob for a while before gently pushing her into the open arms of an older sow. Addressing the crowd now, he spoke, "After much battle, we were able to drive the great serpent off. Your waters are safe once again. No more of your people shall go missing."

The crowd swept him and Ashryn out of the chilly night air into the warm Inn, with cheers and praise and many a pat on his back. *Your secret's safe with me Marlog,* he thought as he sat at a table with a stein of ale and began to spin the tale.

Chapter 5: A Wish For A Dull Moment

Beddigan strolled down a dusty lane in the small village of Wörchen, which was about a two-day trek from his destination of Windermere. He had been taking his time on the journey back to William and his makeshift home, after his encounter at sea with Captain Marlog. He had been keeping a nice, low profile, as to not draw any undue attention from the townspeople in the places he had stayed along the way, taking only the smallest of Adventures to facilitate his journey home.

Though it was only midday, Beddigan decided to stop for the night and stay in Wörchen, which sat just north of Mt. Lileen, along the banks of the Urkna river.

The village was quiet and calm on the sunny afternoon, with most of the townspeople either inside hiding out from the heat, or down by the river cooling off. Salkan lake was a short walk downriver from the town, and a popular spot for relaxing and vacationing in southern Katheyra.

Having entered the town from the north, Beddigan's eyes

were drawn up to the looming mountain in the distance, where he had slain the Dragon Galantus earlier that turning. He couldn't help but smile at the memory of his greatest victory as he sauntered around the village searching for a suitable inn.

Weaving his way through the streets towards the river, he came across The Slumbering Porcupine Inn, which was painted in bright colours like the rest of the buildings in the village, and sported a large wrap around deck, facing the river. He could already see himself settled on one of the plushly padded lounge chairs with a frosty mug of ale, having a spot of rest before returning to regular Adventurer life back in Windermere.

He walked through the bright green swinging double doors of the Inn, into the dim interior. A sleepy old Badger was propped up behind the reception counter and greeted him with a slow nod.

"Hello friend, I am in need of food and lodging for a night," Beddigan requested with a smile.

The old Badger yawned and reached behind him, unhooking a large brass ring with a key on it from a peg board. He tossed it across the counter to Beddigan, "Two gold will get you all you can eat and drink as well as the room."

Beddigan loosened his coin purse and plucked out two gold. It was rather much for a room and food for a night, but this was a popular part of Katheyra and he was happy to pay it for a bit of a break.

The Badger took the gold and tucked it away somewhere below the counter without another word, and then proceeded to lean back in his chair and close his eyes again.

Beddigan shrugged to himself, and turned away, heading up the adjacent stairway. Finding room number seven, which was scratched onto the key, he unlocked it and was pleased to see a small but clean room with bed, table and chair, desk, and washing basin; as well as heavy curtains which shrouded the room in near complete darkness from the midday sun. Tossing his rucksack and sword on to the bed, he tugged the curtains open, blinking rapidly in the light shining through the casement windows. He fiddled with the knobs on the window frame until it popped opened outwardly. He relished the cool air tickling his whiskers. The room faced the river which was only a few yards away across some dusty earth and patchy grass. The azure water churned and foamed over cropping's of rock, and the sandy beaches were spotted with patrons.

After enjoying the view for a few moments, Beddigan changed into his thinner doublet and strapped his sword back on over his breeches, before heading down to the common room. Few tables were occupied as Beddigan weaved his way to the bar.

A short and squat older Badger sow greeted him with a toothy grin. "What'll ya have?" she squawked in the delightful accent of the Badgers of southern Katheyra.

Beddigan smiled, "Ale. And whatever you have for lunch. Can I get it served out to the deck?" he asked. The Badger smiled and nodded pouring his ale and sliding it across the bar to him, before disappearing through a door into what he assumed was the kitchen.

He weaved his way back through the tables, and out into the Inn's foyer. The old Badger who had checked him in was fast asleep and he couldn't help but grin as he stepped lightly past and pushed out of the brightly coloured doors.

The deck was deserted so he chose a chair close to the Inn doors but facing the river, and settled in, sipping his ale.

He could hear the murmur of the water and the occasional reminder of other folks as they shouted at children or called out to one another, but it was still mostly quiet and very peaceful.

"Hi!" Beddigan had just been daydreaming when a small Badger child appeared next to him, young face alight with a grin and dancing, mischievous eyes. "My name's Tolmie, what's yours?"

Beddigan shifted so he was sitting more upright and smiled at the child, "Well hello Tolmie, my name is Beddigan."

Tolmie circled around the chair inspecting him while he answered. "Cool sword. Can I play with it?" the youth asked, his small paws running over the thick leather sheath.

Beddigan smiled, "You remind me of me when I was a young boy, always wanting to touch and play with weapons. I'll tell you what, if your mother says yes, I'll teach you how to swing it properly."

Tolmie stopped moving, his head hung a little lower than before, "I don't have a mum..." he murmured.

Beddigan winced, "I'm sorry to hear that. Who takes care of you then?" he asked the small Badger.

Tolmie scuffed his dusty feet on the wide planks of the deck, "Madam Alissya takes us without parents in."

Beddigan reached into his coin pouch and pulled out a gold piece. The child's eyes grew wide and watched as Beddigan twirled it through his claws.

"Take this gold piece and go have some fun, Tolmie," he flicked the coin into the youth's eager paw.

Tolmie jumped into his lap and hugged him fiercely for a moment, "Thank you Mr. Beddigan!" the little Badger yelped before jumping down and tearing off down the deck, ducking under the railing and disappearing around the side of the building.

Beddigan leaned back in his chair, crossing one leg over the other and sipping his ale. The Inn doors swung open and the squat Badger sow from behind the bar carried his food to him. She set it down on a small side table and Beddigan reached for his coin purse to tip her. His brow furrowed as his paw fumbled for it in its usual place, next to his crystals, only to find the two loose strings it normally hung from. The woman had already turned away, not accustomed to tips it would seem, as Beddigan leapt up from the chair, looking around the deck floor, thinking it had come loose and fallen, but it was nowhere in sight.

Forgetting his food and ale, he raced inside and up the stairs to his room, digging through his belongings jumbled on the bed. Suddenly Tolmie's face flashed in his mind. *That thieving little brat!* he thought, quickly moving back down the stairs.

He banged his fist on the reception counter to wake the old Badger, "Where would I find Madam Alissya?" He snarled.

The old Badger yawned, "This time'a day she'd likely be down at the river with the youngun's. Her place is right by the market, purple house, can't miss it." He said sleepily.

Beddigan thanked him brusquely and stalked out of the Inn, following the dusty trail down to the river's edge.

Once down at the riverbank, he shaded his eyes from the sun and looked up and down the beach for a single female Badger with a bunch of children. It wasn't hard to pick them out as the children were running and jumping around, and racing to and from the water's edge. He made his way through the sand towards the gaggle of children and the single sow laying on a blue beach towel, reading a book. She looked up when his shadow fell across her.

"Excuse me, Madam Alissya?"

The Badger sat up on the towel, "Yes?" she asked, as the children started to slow down and group around them.

Beddigan surveyed them and did not see Tolmie. "A boy named Tolmie, who I believe is under your care, has stolen from me."

The Badger stood up crossing her arms across her chest, "You must be mistaken, Sir. I don't have a boy named Tolmie under my care."

Beddigan frowned, "I won't hurt him, you needn't cover for him. I just want my coin back."

Madam Alissya frowned back at him, "I speak only the truth, *Sir*. Shame on ya for assuming all orphans is thieves!" she growled.

Beddigan stepped back and held up his paws in apology, "I am sorry, madam, I did not mean to imply such things. He told me his name was Tolmie and that he had no mother and that you cared for him. Clearly it was just a part of the ruse. Sorry to bother you."

Before he could turn, she grabbed his forearm, "Wait just a moment. There is a boy... the cloth dyers son. He has claimed to be one of mine before for mischief's sake."

Beddigan nodded and thanked her, hurrying back to the village. She had given him directions to find his way to the cloth dyer's shop and soon he was standing before it, though it was shuttered and closed for the day. He banged on the door several times anyways to no avail. He turned around and almost tripped over the boy, who had crept up right behind him.

"Tolmie!" Beddigan exclaimed as the child giggled and darted a few steps away, "My coin purse, boy. I know you've taken it."

Tolmie grinned, "You must be smart to find where I live so fast! Most people never find me!" the boy giggled again.

Beddigan reached for him, but he darted away again. "This isn't funny, Tolmie. Money is to be earned, and I earned every last coin in that purse."

Tolmie frowned a moment and then reached into the pocket of his pants and retrieved the purse. He tossed it to Beddigan, "I don't steal for tha money. I steal for fun."

Beddigan caught his purse and gave the boy a bewildered look, "And may I ask what is so fun about robbing people?" he questioned.

Tolmie grinned at him, "I always return it, but it's fun ta see how fast and quiet I can be. And how easy it is ta trick folks!"

Beddigan attached his purse to his hip again, and frowned at the boy. "It may feel like fun now, Tolmie, but one day you will steal from someone who will catch you in the act or not be so kind to you when you return it. You won't be a child forever."

Tolmie rolled his eyes in response and took off down the lane yelling back, "Whatever old Mouse!"

Beddigan frowned and made his way back to the Inn, settling in the common room this time as the sun was just starting to dip below the horizon. His belly growled as a reminder that he had missed his lunch. He sipped ale and couldn't help but smile as he remembered a mischievous young Mouse who was always getting into trouble.

Chapter 6: I Ain't Afraid of No Ghost!

Beddigan strolled into Windermere at around midday a couple of days after his vacation in Worchen. He was feeling much more relaxed after the brief respite along the shores of the Urkna River. He had even taken a day to camp along the less popular eastern shore of Salkan Lake on his way back home to Windermere.

Before long he was approaching the cottage that he and William had been staying in. The door opened before he reached it and the lumbering Bear filled the doorway, grinning, "Beddigan T. Mouze! It is about time you returned."

Beddigan smiled back at his dear friend, "Looks as if you have been managing okay in the life of hide or die, in my absence."

They embraced briefly, William chuckling and thumping Beddigan's back hard, and then gesturing for him to come inside. He had sent a message from San Vincent's Port before leaving the city, carefully wording it to let William know that his widow and children were doing well, without ever outright saying as much.

Beddigan tossed his rucksack onto a chair and stretched. William set about gathering some food and ale from the coldbox and setting it at the table while Beddigan stripped out of all but his breeches, wiggling his toes which had desperately needed their freedom from his boots. He slouched in a chair at the table, scrubbing his paws over his face.

William shoved a plate of bread, cheese, and corn across the table to him, as well as a large mug of ale. He drank deeply while William fixed his own plate and sat down across from him at the small dining room table. They ate in silence for a few moments before William met his eyes with a hint of a smile, "Now that you are all rested and relaxed, with a full belly, what say you to an Adventure? The answer better be yes because we leave at sundown."

Beddigan groaned softly and chuckled, "I had hoped at least one night's sleep in a bed, dear friend, though I should have known better. You have never known how to relax."

William grinned over his mug, "The pay is handsome and it isn't too far a trek."

Beddigan nodded, chewing slowly on a hunk of bread, waiting for William to explain the Adventure, but instead the Bear just ate and drank. "Well? What is it that you've committed us to?"

William looked away from Beddigan, suddenly interested only in the ale in his mug.

Beddigan sat up in his chair, narrowing his eyes across the table at his friend, "William," he said in a warning tone, "Tell me."

William cleared his throat, "Well, you see," the Bear hedged, "The village of Pran, just west of here, has somewhat of a mystery on their paws. A whole slew of robberies and a few disappearances as well. The son of the village elder came by searching for help and the villagers sent him my way. His wife is one who has disappeared."

Beddigan nodded along while William continued. "It has been going on for nearly a turning, and happening much more frequently as of late. Lots of folks are damn near broke from the robberies; both money and trade goods."

Beddigan took a final swig of ale and scrubbed his paws over his face again, taking in all that William had said. "And no one has any idea who's behind it all? No eyewitnesses? I mean, by Annalose and Ardra, William! It must be a very talented burglar to get in and out with trade goods and not be seen or heard." He stood, moving to deposit his plate and mug in the wash basin.

William moved to follow suit, as Beddigan made his way to his room, snagging his rucksack from the chair on his way. "Go get cleaned up and repacked. I am going to run grab a few supplies and then we will head out at sundown. Shouldn't take us more than a night to get to Pran." William said as he headed to the front door of the cottage.

Beddigan nodded even though William's back was turned to him, and pumped some water into his washing tub, squeezing his heat crystal to activate it and dunking it in the water. Steam soon billowed into the room as he slipped into the tub to soak his sore muscles.

By the time William returned, Beddigan was dressed in fresh clothing, packed, and sitting on one of the soft chairs in the living area, reading a novel he had picked up in Worchen. Some story written by a noted Badger scholar about the ancient war between the Saints, after Annalose and Ardra divided. He reluctantly tucked the book into his bag and readied himself to leave.

The sun was just starting to dip low in the horizon as William used the last of the natural light to pack up the supplies and his own travel bag. They left their little cottage as the sky turned shades of pink and orange, and by the time they had reached the trail disappearing westward into the forest, they were surrounded by inky darkness.

They walked through the night, stopping in a clearing just off the path to eat and catch a few hours of sleep, and then arrived in Pran mid-morning the following day.

Having never been to Pran, neither Beddigan nor William was expecting such a bustling village. It was larger than they had thought, with a creek running through the centre of town and many rows of cottages and shops. The surrounding area west was broken up into small farm plots where everything from cotton to corn was grown, and to the south orchards of apples and pears stretched off into the horizon.

"Lead the way, friend. We should interview the victims of the robberies, and I would like to speak with the Elder and his son as well," Beddigan said.

When William didn't move forward, Beddigan turned to look at him, brow furrowed, "What? What is it?"

William cleared his throat, "Uhh, well, you see..." he trailed off, avoiding eye contact.

Beddigan crossed his arms across his chest, frowning, "What aren't you telling me, William?" he asked in a hard voice.

William sighed, "I sort of left out a part of the story. It is not so much that the victims haven't a clue who stole their belongings..."

Beddigan's eyebrows shot up, "Okay... and? If we know who we are looking for that will make things a lot easier."

William winced, "Yes... except that it isn't just one that we are looking for; it is a group. And they aren't exactly... easy to find."

Beddigan threw his paws up in the air, "Annalose and Ardra, William! Just spit it out!"

William sighed again, "Okay, okay! The victims that have seen the robberies firsthand, of which there are several, as well as bystanders that have witnessed these burglaries... they have all seen friends and family members who have been long dead looting their goods. In the form of... ghosts."

Beddigan's mouth hung open for a moment. He cleared his throat, "And you didn't tell me this very important detail because you knew I wouldn't have come. Smart Bear."

William winced again as Beddigan paced back and forth angrily, "Look, they need our help as much as anyone else. You know how devoutly religious Southern Katheyra is. They are too scared to approach or follow the ghosts. It is a perfect job for us."

Beddigan frowned at him for a moment and then sighed, "I don't like it. But we are committed. Now, let's go have a chat with these folks and see if we can figure out what in this Warbler's Cursed world is going on here."

***

After meeting with the Elder and his son Jakob, and several of the victims throughout most of the day, Beddigan and William checked into the Burping Billy Goat Inn. Ordering dinner to be sent up to their room, they settled in at the little table by the window, their bags piled on each of the two single beds occupying most of the room's space and began to discuss their findings.

As William had reminded him, Southern Katheyran's were quite religious, which was a bit of a culture shock for Beddigan, coming from the much less religious Illensdar. The conversations had been scored by the clashing of their beliefs. William handled the devout Badgers much better, as religion was a strong aspect of life in Sinerrah as well, and he was used to it. Deep believers in reincarnation and cyclical life, several of the victims were convinced that their loved one's spirits needed the goods and coin and were not willing to help with the investigation at all.

The most cooperative were the ones whose family members had gone missing, like Jakob's wife, though several of the robbery victims were convinced those that were missing were called to the next life by their kin. It had been frustrating to try and speak with them all and get details about each individual case because of the religious rhetoric and arguing that commenced.

"Any ideas?" William asked, sipping from his mug of spiced pear cider, a local delicacy, that he had snagged from the common room on their way upstairs.

Beddigan looked up from his mug which he had been staring into absentmindedly, "Well, we know it isn't actual spirits, or ghosts. But beyond that, all I can think of is that it must be some sort of mass hallucination. Maybe poison in the water wells? Or some sort of sorcery?"

William nodded, "But if it were the water then everybody would be reporting seeing the ghosts and so far, that is not the case."

Beddigan nodded, "Good point. Sorcery then. Hooray..." he

said dryly.

William couldn't help but chuckle. Beddigan groaned to himself. Aside from crystals, which were becoming a bit of a mystery all their own with his recent encounters, magic potential was a rare trait. A large part of the reason that Mormant had conquered Reene and continued to keep a firm paw on their people and population, was because of their fear of the historically strong magical potential in the Reenal people. Mormant had the least magical potential among their lands, and Illensdar close after. Sinerrah was somewhere near the middle of the road between most and least, though no one really knew except the Bears themselves, as they kept it a closely guarded national secret.

It was said by historians that the inhabitants of the Rainier Island were all born with magical potential, which would explain why their country was closed from the rest of the land by the mysterious, impenetrable fog, but again there wasn't much evidence of that. And as for Katheyra, most of their potential was relegated to Seers in the north and priests and priestesses in the south. It wasn't common to come across a sorcerer Badger that didn't fall into one of those two categories.

A knock at the door signalled their food had arrived and Beddigan answered it, letting the stout Badger waddle in and set the tray on the table. They both inhaled deeply the rich aroma of the hearty vegetable stew in front of them and began to eat in silence.

Suddenly William made a strangled sound and his spoon clattered to the table. Beddigan's head snapped up as he looked at his friend who was coughing heavily, "William, are you all right?!" he stood quickly, his chair scraping across the wooden planks of the floor, falling backwards with a crash as he raced around and thumped hard on the Bear's back. William raised a shaking paw and pointed out the window. Beddigan's eyes rounded and his eyebrows shot up as he saw several gauzy, white apparitions floating down the main street outside the Inn.

They both stared at the throng of ghosts until they had disappeared beyond sight. William cleared his throat, "We're sure we don't believe in ghosts, right?"

Beddigan swallowed hard, "Yes. Certainly not ghosts," but the raised hair on his arms and neck betrayed him

***

Beddigan ushered William through the front door of the Inn and into the darkness outside, pulling the door shut quietly behind him. After a moment of hesitation, they had shaken away their spike of fear and raced down the stairs. As the door clicked shut softly behind them, Beddigan winced, "Get a hold over yourself!" he whispered to himself.

William was close ahead of him, as they waited a moment for their eyes to adjust to the darkness. The Bear turned back to Beddigan and whispered, "Have you ever seen a ghost before?"

Beddigan shook his head, "And I still haven't. Ghosts aren't real, William. It is just a trick of sorcery," William nodded but the look in his friend's eyes showed more fear than anything else. Beddigan braced a paw on the large Bear's back. "A well-done trick of sorcery, I'll admit, but you've nothing to fear, my friend. Now let's get going or we may lose them."

The two of them moved quickly in the shadows, hugging close to buildings along the road until they crested over the slight hill that led outside of the village and down into the orchards.

They ducked low at the edge of the path and watched as the apparitions dispersed among the fruit trees. They quickly lost track of the ghostly forms, leaving them crouched in the dirt, looking down at the quiet fruit trees.

William stood up first, "Well, now what do we do? We have no clue where they have gone."

Beddigan stood alongside his friend, turning back towards the village. His mouth froze open as he began to answer William's question. William noticed his friend's pause and whirled around, paw moving to his new, un-engraved dagger.

There, smack-dab in the middle of the pathway, only a few meters away from them, was the ghostly specter of an older Mouse soldier. The semi- transparent sash denoted him to be a Captain of Her Majesty's Royal Sapphire Brigade. The ghost floated slowly towards them. William took several steps back on the pathway, nearly falling backwards down the slope towards the orchards, but Beddigan was frozen in place. Stopping inches from Beddigan's face, the ghost spoke in a hollow voice, "Hello my son." Beddigan's mouth still hung open, and he worked to close it, to clear his dry throat and speak.

William's voice came from behind him before he could form words with his mouth once again, "He is not your papa, Beddigan. It is just a trick, remember?"

Swallowing hard, Beddigan stared into the ghostly rendition of his father's face, which he had not seen since he was just a child. He blinked away the tears forming in his eyes, and thought, *William is right. This is not your father. It isn't any part of him. This is a trick of sorcery meant to distract you.*

He cleared his throat, "Whoever or whatever you are, you are no part of my father." He spoke clearly; thankful his voice didn't waver.

The ghost's face didn't shift in acknowledgement of his words at all, until it spoke again, "Perhaps your mother would be more to your liking." In a bright shimmer the apparition rearranged into a perfect picture of his mother.

Beddigan's breath caught in his throat, "Mama," he whispered. Her ghostly paw reached out to caress his cheek, though he felt nothing on his fur, his heart thumped heavily in his chest. Suddenly he was pushed out of the way, tripping over his feet and landing on the side of the dirt path.

"Don't you touch him! You are not his Mama," William roared.

For a moment, Beddigan caught an odd distortion of the features of his mother's face, a smile much too wide and a sharpening of the eyes, and then POOF! It was gone, and William was left snarling at nothing at all.

Beddigan stood, brushing himself off, moving to William's side, and patting the Bear's back, which was still trembling from the encounter.

"Thank you, friend. We are definitely dealing with some powerful sorcery and I can see why so many of the villagers were willing to allow these ghosts into their homes," he said, the fur on the back of his neck and forearms still bristling. They headed back to the Inn in silence. William seemed more angry than scared now, which heartened Beddigan's resolve to sort out this mess and bring those responsible to justice.

***

The following morning, they rose early to take breakfast in the common room, hoping to hear news of what the ghosts had gotten up to the night before while they were clearly being distracted. The common room was quiet though, leaving them alone with their porridge and tea.

Once they had finished eating, they headed to the village Elder's home and walked right into several villagers offering their complaints of robberies the night before. This time, however, all the Badger's affected were convinced it was foul play, and not their loved ones at all. Like Beddigan had witnessed firsthand the night before, the apparitions had seemed very real and spot on to who they were supposed to be, until there was a flicker; just a mere moment of something else.

These reports were the first of this nature to the Elder, who thanked the villagers for their reports and dismissed them. Beddigan and William sat down in the Elder's living room, on a couch much too small for the Bear's bulk, just as the Elder's son Jakob joined them.

"What do you make of it?" Jakob asked.

Beddigan recounted their story from the night before and then continued, "I think the sorcerer behind this never had to split his or her concentration as they did last night, and it ended up weakening the apparitions, allowing a bit of themselves to shine through."

Jakob nodded along, "You didn't get enough of a look to know who may be behind it all though?" the Badger questioned.

Beddigan shook his head, "Unfortunately not. It was so quick, just a fleeting moment, really."

Jakob made a frustrated sound and hopped to his feet to pace the room, "So, we really aren't any closer to getting my wife back then."

William spoke up, "We at least know what to expect now."

Beddigan nodded to William, "He's right, Jakob. We needed to know what to expect, and now we just need to find out who is behind it all. I know I have asked this before, but is there anyone at all you could think of that maybe has a grudge against the village or even your father?"

Jakob thought a moment and then sat down next to the Elder with a sigh, "No, there isn't anyone at all. Everyone loves my father, and he has done a great job as Elder of Pran."

After a few more minutes of repeated questioning, Beddigan excused William and himself, assuring the Elder and Jakob that they would come up with a plan to expose who was behind this trickery.

The pair wandered the streets of the village looking for signs of a suspicious nature until William's stomach growls became audible enough that they stopped in the Inn's common room for lunch. Over bowls of steaming soup and crusty, dark bread, they discussed their options, settling on a stake out of the wealthiest of the Badgers in the village that had not yet been robbed or plagued by the ghosts of loved ones. They would wait in hiding and follow the apparitions once they had looted the resident, letting them lead the way to whoever was behind it all.

Once they had finished eating, they returned to their room to sleep until dusk. Shortly after the sun had ducked behind the horizon, they left the Inn and proceeded to the wealthier area of the village where the owner of several of the orchards lived in a sprawling home with his family. He had agreed to the stakeout as long as the Elder was willing to shelter his wife and children for the night.

By the time Beddigan and William arrived, a sole lamp lit up the living room, as visible through the large bay window in the front of the house, with just the single Badger sitting alone, reading by the fire.

Crouched behind a neighbouring house, Beddigan peered around the corner, waiting for the apparitions to arrive. William was in a similar position next to the house on the opposite side of their target, hoping that with both of the vantage points covered, they wouldn't miss the robbery.

It didn't take long before Beddigan spotted the wavering ghost of an older Badger sow appear directly in front of the house, before floating up the broad steps and through the closed front door. Signaling to William to join him, they dashed across the street to hide in the shadows next to the stairs of the house.

Before long the apparition was floating back down the steps, its ghostly arms loaded with bags of coin and jewelry.

Beddigan was puzzled at the sight, remembering the ghostly paw of his mother seemingly touching his cheek, though he felt nothing of his fur. *How is it carrying things but can float through a solid wood door?* he thought.

Filing that question away for later he followed the apparition through the town, from shadow to shadow, with William close behind. They crept along the path that led out into the patches of farmland, struggling to keep pace and not lose sight of the swiftly moving ghost.

The apparition veered off down a wagon-rutted side road that led to a big, ramshackle barn. The land around it was overgrown and clearly hadn't been tilled in many turnings. Beddigan crouched behind a tree not far from the barn doors and watched the ghost floating inside, the bags or loot mysteriously shimmering through the solid wood.

Turning to ask William what he thought was the best way to

proceed now that they had indeed found the root of the sorcery, he found nothing but still, night air behind him. William was gone.

***

Beddigan swore under his breath, backtracking up the wagon-ruts to the main road. "William!" he called softly, but urgently, turning around in a full circle; eyes sharp for any indication of the Bear's large form. Sighing, he turned back to the barn, which sat still and silent in the night.

"Lost another friend I see, Beddigan," tutted an eerie voice from behind him.

He whirled about, paw on the hilt of his sword. His paw dropped to his side as the air puffed out of his lungs. There, just a few feet away from him, was his oldest, dearest friend from his time in Her Majesty's Royal Sapphire Brigade: Sir Charrin. Beddigan shook his head, eyes wide as saucers, "N-no. No," he stammered, "*You aren't real*," he hissed, as much to himself as to the ghost.

The apparition chuckled softly, "Aren't I though? I mean look here," the apparition unbuttoned his semi-transparent tunic and pulled it apart revealing a grisly scar on his chest, "I still have this souvenier of your betrayal of Her Majesty... and your friends."

Beddigan gasped as the shame that always lived within him bloomed anew. His paw trembled as he struggled to remain rooted in reality. "You can't fool me," he said in a shaking voice, "I do not know how you are doing this, but I do know you are *not* Sir Charrin, the same way you weren't my mother or my father."

The apparition's face shifted slightly before resolving back to Sir Charrin's likeness. "I owe you something, Beddigan. And I think it's time I returned it." The apparition drew a dagger from a scabbard slung around its hips. Even in its translucent form, Beddigan recognized is at his very own, having last seen in when it was plunged to hilt into Charrin's chest. In the flash of gold and sapphire, the dagger shifted from ethereal, nearly transparent shades of white and blue, to hard and cold gold and steel. The sapphire jewels encrusting the hilt sparkled in the moonlight.

Before Beddigan could draw his sword, the ghost flew forward, slashing at his chest with the dagger. Throwing his arm up to block, Beddigan felt the blade sink into his flesh. The ghost was fast; too fast to block, and it slashed again, this time deep into his shoulder.

Ducking away, Beddigan drew his sword and swung it at the ghost, watching in awe as it sailed through its translucent form. The dagger slashed again, catching his thigh, causing him to yelp and fall to his knees. Looking up at the face of his long-gone friend, he saw the same obscure stretching of the smile, the sharp teeth, and the wicked gleam in the eyes that he had seen take over his mother's face the night before. The dagger drew back, and fell hard on Beddigan's head, hilt first. He felt himself falling to the ground on his back as his vision darkened. His last glimpse was of Sir Charrin, face distorted in laughter, with the dagger fading in his paw.

***

Beddigan awoke, stifling a groan as he gathered his bearings. His head pounded, and he fought the dizziness that was blurring his limited vision in the dark. He was tied to a chair with his paws bound behind him and feet secured to each chair leg. The chair was much too small for his frame, leaving his knees bent at an awkward angle, adding to the pain he already felt from the dagger slashes and bludgeoning. His eyes adjusted a bit to the darkness and he peered around for signs of anyone or anything else. A small sigh of relief released from his lungs, unbidden, at the lack of any ethereal forms.

Unfortunately, he also saw no large, dark shadows to indicate William was tied up alongside him. By the shape of the beams and the smell of moldy hay, Beddigan was sure he was inside the ramshackle barn. There were several woven sacks piled around the floor, along with larger crates tucked against the walls.

Though it was too dark to tell their contents, he suspected that they held the stolen goods of the villagers of Pran.

His ears perked up at the creaking sound of a rusty hinge. He searched along the walls of the barn for where the door may be but couldn't determine in the dark where it was or wasn't. The hint of a cool breeze tickled the fur at the base of his neck, confirming that the door had definitely opened, and that it was at his back. Something brushed against his arm, fluid with the darkness; barely a shimmering distortion of the air around him. A distant echoing of soft laughter grew louder as the breeze picked up in the room, swirling bits of hay into the air, and raising enough dust to set Beddigan off in a coughing fit.

A flash of bright orange light blinded his teary eyes, leaving him blinking rapidly as the wind died off. As his vision cleared, the light in the room rose into a dull orange glow like that of lamplight, though he could not see any lamp or torch, nor smell the pungent liquid used for fuel.

As if stepping through a door he could not see, a hooded figure appeared just in front of him, with long, sweeping robes brushing over the dirty floor. The hood was drawn up high enough to shade the figure's face completely from Beddigan's view. "One can only assume you are the sorceress behind this whole mess?" Beddigan growled, his voice rough from coughing.

The breathy chuckle he had heard before emerged from the cloak, "You are much smarter than these pitiful Katheyran's. I knew you would be trouble the moment I saw you here." The figure moved around the room slowly, in large, pacing, serpentine motions, "You see, I am quite familiar with your work, *Sir* Beddigan."

Beddigan sighed, "What have you done with William?" He watched as the figure's fluid movements hitched for a just moment and then continued.

"William is no more a concern of yours, or anyone really. And soon you will suffer the same fate." The figure stopped, facing him, though still far enough away that despite straining he couldn't make out the face within the hood, "You brought this on yourself. I tried to warn you off, but you had to be gallant and heroic and try to save these poor wretches from the big, bad, sorceress. I can't have you meddling in my affairs any more than these dimwits could have figured this out themselves."

Beddigan's heart sank. *William...* he thought blinking back tears at the thought of his dear, lost friend.

He looked up, a vicious snarl contorting his face as anger washed away sadness. He searched once again for a face beneath the darkness of the figure's hood to focus his anger upon. "You best be quick about it then, sorceress, because if I get out of these bonds you will pay for what you have done," he growled.

The hooded figure laughed, this time a much heartier and shrill sound. With a swift movement, the arms of the near shapeless figure swept the hood back, causing Beddigan to gasp. Shianne grinned at him, a feral light flickering in her eyes. "You were a fool to ever trust me, and now it will be your ultimate undoing, Beddigan," she sneered, pulling the jeweled dagger from the sleeve of her cloak, the same one that the apparition wearing Sir Charrin's face had struck him with earlier.

Beddigan narrowed his eyes at Shianne and opened his mouth to speak when something occurred to him: Shianne seemed taller. *Maybe it's just because I am on such a small chair*, he thought. But that wasn't all. Her eyes seemed... wrong. And her fur was back to its tell-tale Fox red-gold. *Why would she change it back when she had such a great disguise*, he thought.

She moved toward him gracefully, gripping the dagger.

"You don't have to do this," Beddigan breathed out, mind working in overdrive, trying to sort a way out of this mess he was in. He rolled his wrists trying to loosen the bonds but had no luck in freeing his paws.

"But I do. You are a loose thread that needs to be cut. Any last words, Beddigan?" she all but whispered.

Beddigan's jaw worked but no words came to him. He looked up, meeting her eyes. He was about to say his final piece when he caught a shift in the dark corner of the barn behind her. A large shape moved out from the shadows, and the figure of Shianne caught the widening in Beddigan's eyes and turned. With a crash, the cloaked figure collapsed to the ground, the dagger skidding across the dirt floor. To Beddigan's relief, William stood in her wake, clutching a heavy gold statue of the god Ardra in one of his giant paws.

"William! You're a sight for sore eyes! She said she'd killed you!"

William dropped the statue with a thump and rushed over, snagging the dagger from the ground and using it to free Beddigan from his restraints.

He stood on wobbly legs, sore from the cramped position and the dagger slashes from the earlier fight, which marred his breeches with sticky, red patches.

The friends briefly embraced, William gripping his shoulders, "Annalose and Ardra! Beddigan T. Mouze, I swear you have nine lives."

Beddigan chuckled, "A few moments more and I wouldn't have any life at all. Thank you, dear friend."

William nodded, his eyes sliding up over Beddigan's shoulder to the pile of cloak on the ground, "I knew we couldn't trust that one, I told you as much before."

Beddigan turned and crouched down by the heap of cloth. He peered, gingerly lifting the hood that had settled over the figure's head. As he suspected, it no longer bore the shiny red fur of the people of Reene, nor the delicate features of his old friend Shianne. "Ahh William, but this isn't anyone we've met before."

William's eyes flew wide with shock, "But she was not a ghost! She was solid. She was that crazy Shianne... I *know* she was. I saw it with my own eyes!"

Beddigan nodded to his friend, "Looks can be deceiving," he said simply, "Especially when sorcery is involved."

Pulling back the cloak with a flourish, he rolled the figure onto its back. There, framed against the dirt floor, was a creature that Beddigan had only seen in books, and that William had never seen at all. Delicate gray fur with black stripes, and long silver whiskers; with slanted almond eyes and wide, tufted ears. A slender, long frame with delicate paws, clearly housing razor sharp claws, and small pink nose.

"What in the name of this Warbler's Cursed world is that?!" William exclaimed.

Beddigan gingerly took the pulse of the still figure, finding a steady heartbeat, before replying, "She is one of the Lynx people... from The Ranier Islands. And clearly a very powerful sorceress."

William gawked a few moments, speechless, and rightfully so. There hadn't even been reports of seeing a Lynx on either continent in ages. Clearing his throat, the Bear asked, "Well... what do we do with her?"

Beddigan stood back up and limped around her to the sacks and crates piled around the room, beckoning William to join him.

"I'm certain the missing items of the Katheyran's are amongst these bags and boxes. I haven't a clue what to do with her or even how to restrain her," Beddigan said, thoughtfully.

William began digging through the boxes and bags, happy to have at least found the stolen goods.

Beddigan turned back to check on the Lynx and gasped.

William spun around, "Where did she go?!" the Bear yelped.

Beddigan hobbled as quickly as he could to the barn door, which was swinging open in the night air. The Lynx was staggering up the wagon-rutted path but stopped and turned back as she heard the Bear and Mouse exit the barn, "Oh, give it up you two! You can't stop me; you can't restrain me... take solace in the fact that I'm too injured to kill you."

Beddigan crossed his arms across his chest, "We can't just let you leave here after tormenting these folks."

The Lynx chuckled again, "You think I fear you, Mouse? You are but an annoying gnat nipping at me. Your lumbering oaf partner may have gotten the better of me this time, but next time, should you disrupt my plans again, I will see to it that you both find very deep graves." And with that she disappeared.

William ran up the path to where she had been standing, only to find nothing at all. Beddigan strained his eyes in the night for the shimmering distortion he had seen before, but there was no sign of it.

William walked back down the path to him, "Well, that's that, I guess. For now. At least we have the villagers' things to give back to them," he muttered.

Beddigan nodded absentmindedly, as he stared into the night. This wasn't going to be their last encounter with the Lynx sorceress. He could feel it in his bones.

Chapter 7: Barely Beddigan

Shianne shut the door of her luxurious room at the Wriggling Walrus Inn, found in the wealthy, western quarter of San Vincent's Port. She leaned back against it for a moment, closing her eyes and breathing out a carefully contained sigh of relief. She only allowed herself to feel relief for a few seconds at a time, only when she was alone and behind closed doors. In her line of work, she had to stay sharp, alert; ready for anything. But after a day, and a job like the one she'd just had, she needed that brief respite before she could set her mind right again.

She strode across the spacious room to the small, solid oak table and chairs nestled underneath a large window. She quickly tugged the drapes closed, making a mental note to never stay in this Inn again, as the staff had not followed her specific instructions to have all drapes drawn before her arrival.

She unhooked her belt and laid it on the table, unhindered by the streaks of tacky, not quite dried blood that her splattered daggers left upon the wood.

She pulled a chair out and sat, perching on the edge of it, leaning down to unlace her knee-high boots. They too had spots of blood on them, marring the shiny black leather. She sighed, more out of frustration than anything else. She placed the boots on the table, adding streaks of dirt and clumps of dark, crumbly mud to the mess, and moved barefoot across the plush carpet to the adjoining washing room.

Gathering a small basin from a shelf, she filled it with crystal-warmed water and soap, and grabbed a stack of plush white cloths, carrying them back to the table. After grabbing her leather polish from the small bag that she had left by the door, she set about cleaning and shining her weapons and boots. Despite her clothing being splattered with muck and blood as well, she only ever meticulously cleaned her tools; not only because she had but one set of each with her while she traveled, but because they deserved more reverence than the mere cloth that shielded her fur from weather and eyes. She couldn't help but smile as she swirled one of the cloths in the warm water. A major perk to staying in a posh Inn was having warm water from the pump. Not that it was much of a job to heat water with a crystal, but it was still easier this way after a long day.

A loud ding signaled her food being sent up via a dumbwaiter in the corner of the room. Another perk was not having to interact with anyone, which was definitely a major plus to an assassin.

The day had been long. Several times her plans had been derailed as she tailed the Badger she had been paid a handsome sum to make disappear; a former gang member who had defected to another gang and was sharing too much information about his old comrades. He knew that his former associates would be sending someone for him, so he had been careful to never be alone. He had even brought members from the new gang along with him for protection.

Normally, this sort of job was preferable to Shianne; not that she cared much about the target generally, but killing scum was just easier. And more pleasant. She had learned early in the assassin game that you can't be picky about jobs. But with the lengths she'd had to go to to get her target alone had been frustrating, and she'd ended up having to take out several other people that she had not been paid to bother with. It wasn't solely the money that bothered her; it was the effort, and the needless death. Many perceived her to be an unhinged, heartless killing machine, but she didn't like wasteful death any more than the next person.

Once everything was clean and polished, she strapped her belt back on with her daggers safely in their scabbards, leaving her boots on the table. She retrieved her food from the dumbwaiter and sat down cross-legged on the plush carpet with her back against the wall, next to the table and across from the door. She didn't like that the wall had a window on it, but the room didn't give many other options. She inhaled the herbed aroma of the stew that was tucked into a large ball of bread, shaped like a bowl.

"Fleeting moments of pleasure in a world of death," she murmured to herself. It had become like a mantra to her over the years and helped her to distance herself a bit from what she had become. Pieces of her were broken, but little moments like this made her feel whole again.

She sat and ate until there was barely a crumb left. She left the ale she had ordered untouched, but sipped the water that had come along with her dinner. She never drank the ale, but ordering it served as a way to make her order seem commonplace. Assassins, in general, never wanted to stand out, but Shianne especially needed a solid cover at all times. Whole countries would love her dead or imprisoned, so she couldn't be too careful.

Despite her day being long and tiring, after shoving her dishes back into the dumbwaiter, the ale poured down the drain of the washing tub, she changed into a fresh tunic and breeches and slipped her boots back on. She didn't sleep well on the best of days, but this day had left her particularly restless.

She slipped quietly out of her room and down the hallway to the private stairs for the luxury floor of the Inn. It wasn't terribly late yet, but the sky outside was dark. The moon shone brightly illuminating the patches of the cobble stone roadway that fell outside of the streetlamps flickering light. She meandered through the streets of the western quarter, moving closer to the still bustling inner circle of the city.

She wandered through the night markets for quite some time, browsing and people watching, the hood of her clock pulled up against the chilly night air. She soon found herself heading into the rougher eastern quarter of the city to an old haunt. Her dear friend Alizan ran the quiet drinking house near the outer wall, quite close to the southern quarter. It had been a while since she had visited, so when she spotted the dull light coming from the older stone building's windows she felt a spark of excitement. She slipped in and settled at the far end of the long bar. At the late hour, only a few tables were occupied with patrons, all looking like those of various levels of disrepute.

A tall, striking Bear sow moved over to serve her, "What'll ya have?"

Shianne reached up and swept her hood off, grinning, "Honey-wine and a hug?"

The Bear reached across and pulled Shianne nearly half over the bar in a crushing hug, "Lass! It's been too long!"

Shianne wiggled back to her seat while Alizan moved to get her the drink she had ordered. The Bear slid the drink in front of her, "Wait here just for a moment. I'll be right back."

Shianne nodded, letting the heat from the delicately warmed, amber liquid warm her paws. She was just taking her first sip when Alizan returned, thunking a heavy stack of worn envelopes tied together with twine down on the bar.

Shianne's eyes widened, "All from him?" she asked.

Alizan nodded, "I told ya it'd been too long," the Bear answered with a snort.

Shianne winced a bit, "Sorry Ali, you know how it is..." she murmured, slipping a dagger free and slicing through the twine. She leafed through the envelopes, sealed with the prim and proper red wax seal of one Beddigan T. Mouze.

"It's alright deary, just glad you're here now," Alizan said, reaching out to pat Shainne's cheek. "Bottom one just came in a few days ago."

Shianne set aside the older envelopes and used her claw to open the newest. The thick parchment was of good quality and smelled like the berry- toned ink that was written upon it.

Dear Shianne,

I hope this letter finds you well. As usual, I don't expect you to write me back, though I do have some questions for you. A lot of questions, actually, and getting answers is becoming increasingly important.

I'm sure you can imagine the questions you left me with after our last encounter. As curious as I am about what I saw and what you hinted at, a much more serious situation has arisen.

William and I were called to help a little village with a ghostly thieving problem, which ended up being the result of some very powerful sorcery. I am not just talking about apparitions to cause fear, Shianne, but to replicate loved ones long gone. And they knew things; things that no one could know but me. The sorcerer was able to read minds or memories, and was able to shape-shift. She took your form and nearly killed me.

Once William had knocked her out, we were able to see her true form. Shianne, she was a Lynx. And after what I saw of you last, you may be the only one with any information about her, or her people.

The crime this time was petty, but with the power she displayed is extremely disconcerting.

I hope you may have some answers for me. Perhaps we can arrange a meeting soon, provided you are still in Katheyra. You know where to find me.

Sincerely,

Beddigan T. Mouze

Shianne read the letter, took a sip of her honey-wine, and then read the letter again. She was careful not to let her anger curl her claws through the parchment. Beddigan was right to ask her these questions, though she wasn't sure she would answer them. His intuition was spot on, as usual. Taking a final sip of her honey-wine, she folded the letter and tucked it into her lapel.

"And just like that I've got to run. Would you mind holding these a bit longer, Ali?" she asked with an apologetic smile.

The Bear frowned but nodded, tucking the box behind the bar. Shianne walked around the bar and hugged her friend one last time, then tugged her hood up and slinked out into the night.

Most of the lamps on the street were out due to the late hour so she moved quickly back to the inner circle where she knew a few would still be lit. She carefully pulled an onyx crystal from a small leather pouch hooked to the inner portion of her cloak. She held it and focused her mind until the crystal warmed in her paw. Placing it back in the pouch, she headed east.

Though the East Gate out of the city was closed to travellers at this time of night, you could still leave the city through a one-way gate. She slipped through it without the city guards even noticing her.

Once outside the city she moved through the darkness, swift and silent until she entered the thick forest. Her eyes adjusted as she picked her way through the trees, remaining well off the main road, and checking periodically to make sure she was not being followed. She finally came to a little path that led to a clearing she'd had many meetings in before. She saw a brief distortion in the air as she moved towards the center of the clearing. A silvery ring of light appeared, and a cloaked figure stepped through. Shianne approached, fishing her light crystal out of her pouch, and setting it to its brightest setting.

"You had best have a very good reason for calling me here, Whisper," the figure growled, pushing the hood of its cloak down. The light from the crystal illuminated the soft grey and black striped fur of a Lynx sorceresses face.

Shianne kept walking until she was almost touching the Lynx. She gripped its arms through the cloak, digging her claws in painfully, "That's Death's Whisper, to you *Valenceena*," she snarled with a feral smile.

The Lynx took a step back, "Unhand me immediately!" she shrieked.

Shianne let go and took a step back.

"The nerve," the sorceress growled, "I have no fear of you, *whelp*."

Shianne watched the Lynx, noticing the quick pace with which she breathed, "You should," Shianne said softly.

The Lynx made a frustrated sound, "Enough with the theatrics! What is it that you want?"

Shianne crossed her arms across her chest, "You knew the deal when I helped smuggle you out of the Islands; do as you please but don't get caught. And I hear you failed handsomely with the latter."

Valenceena's eyes flashed with rage, "That wasn't my fault," she spat out, "It was that damn Mouse adventurer and his oaf Bear friend! I made it very clear to them that should we cross paths again they will no longer walk this plane."

Shianne chuckled softly, shaking her head slowly, "And what is to keep them from telling everyone what they have seen?"

Valenceena waived her paw dismissively, "Bah, who would believe such things? They would be considered crazy far before others would believe a Lynx was in Katheyra." Shianne was silent in response. Valenceena had begun pacing and suddenly stopped, "Wait. How did you hear of this?"

Shianne's feral smile returned, "The Mouse is very important to my plans."

Eyes dilatating slightly, and a ghost of smile across her mouth, Valenceena replied, "Ahh, is it smart to reveal such a weakness then?"

Shianne flew across the space between them, quicker than a heartbeat, a dagger out and poised at the sorceress's throat before Valenceena could even move. "You will leave him out of it. You will wear your disguise and you will *never* presume to threaten me again," Shianne growled. The Lynx gulped hard, barely nodding.

Shianne waited a moment before releasing her, sheathing her dagger and turning to walk away. Her keen senses told her never to turn her back on anything or anyone, but the confidence the gesture radiated suited the moment. She felt the heat before she saw the ball of fire go sailing past her face, singing the edges of the fur on her cheeks. She whirled around with a snarl.

"You think too highly of yourself, Whisper," Valenceena sneered, "I could end you this moment. You may be strong and fast, but you have no power compared to I."

Shianne grinned, paw rubbing her burned cheek, "You underestimate *me*, Valenceena. I am more than fast and strong. I am smarter than you, and infinitely more ruthless. You are spoiled by your power."

Valenceena's face twisted into a cruel mask, "You insult me and expect to live. I call *that* very stupid."

Another fireball hurtled towards Shianne, which she easily side-stepped, moving closer to the Lynx. "I could end you at any time, Valenceena. You know this to be true, yet you put on this show, this spectacle! I do not fear you. I will never fear you."

Shianne took a few more steps towards the sorceress, "And I have some very powerful allies that would love to know what I know about getting to and from the Ranier Islands. You wouldn't want Wolves at your family's doorstep now, would you?"

Anger slowly faded from the Lynx's face, as the words sunk in. She lowered her paw, "I will leave the Mouse alone," she said, shakily.

Shianne stopped in front of her and patted Valenceena's cheek, "There's a good girl. Now go before I lose my temper with you."

The Lynx nodded, stumbling as she stepped backwards, hurrying to summon the portal. She stepped through the shimmering oval hastily and disappeared.

Shianne watched until the slivery light was eclipsed by the darkness of the night before letting a soft breath out. Stuck out of the city for the night, she laid down on the grass, looking up at the night sky littered with stars. "You're welcome, Beddigan," she murmured.

Chapter 8: Treason Most Foul

Beddigan cringed as the carriage slid down into a deep rut in the road, causing him to roll and thump against the hard, wooden seat. He had been inside the small, stuffy carriage for nearly a day, deciding to forgo another day or two of walking in the interest of arriving in San Vincent's Port as soon as possible. He had been heading to the city from Windermere when he had received a message that the Republic Council needed his services urgently.

Katheyra, being a people's republic, had an elected council of representatives from all over the country; from the Snowcap mountain range to the hard-baked earth of the Southern flatlands. The representatives gathered for the majority of each turning in the capital city of San Vincent's Port, where in lieu of a palace like Illensdar or Mormant, there was a Council House near the center of the inner-city ring.

Beddigan had done occasional jobs for council members over his time as an Adventurer, but never had he received one of the golden sealed summons requests that had found him while he was still a few days' walk southeast of the city. He had hired passage on the first inexpensive carriage he had come across and almost immediately regretted it, as both tail and bottom were sore in minutes.

With a great sigh of relief, Beddigan perked up as the roadway became increasingly clogged with pedestrians and wagons. Tapping the driver to stop, he paid the full fare and nodded his thanks before jumping down on wobbly legs and completing the journey by foot.

Before long he was being processed through the bustling East Gate of the city. He stepped forward to the first of the many guards that all travellers needed to be vetted by. The guard he approached was a Bear of considerable size, likely to intimidate those that may be looking to enter the city for nefarious means. He handed over his summons request, hoping to expedite the process and was pleased when the Bear's eyebrows shot up and he was escorted immediately through the gate and passed off to a Council House attendant who had been waiting nearby; a Badger small of stature but trembling with a tremendous sense of urgency.

The little Badger barely spoke as he led Beddigan swiftly through the throngs of people to the inner circle, where the market was packed with travellers and merchants. Having spent much time in the city, Beddigan knew exactly how to get to the Council House, but indulged his guide as they swerved and dodged around apple carts and tapestry kiosks to the western edge of the market. The stalls thinned out and the people came in fewer numbers as the dusky pink sandstone building came into view.

Squatting on the edge of the market, near the road that led to the western quarter and the West Gate, the Council House boasted three stories, casting a large shadow across the well-packed earth pathways of the market square. It had low, wide stairs leading up to the grand entrance, and white columns hoisting up the slight overhang of the roof. Shiny brass ringed the many windows and adorned the doors leading inside the building.

Not only did the Council House stand as the seat of power in Katheyra, but it also served as the residences for the representatives when the council was in session. Around the sides and back of the building were carefully maintained gardens with lush grass, cobblestone pathways, and patches of brightly coloured flowers.

Despite all the time he had spent in San Vincent's Port recently, he had not been inside of the Council House in many turnings. As the attendant led him inside and brought him through the beautifully maintained white stone interior of the lobby, he couldn't help but be struck a bit by the splendor. He was ushered into a dimly lit antechamber filled with plush red chairs and told to wait. He sat down, relishing the squishy soft cushion against his still tender tail and bottom.

He had been sitting for quite some time when the attendant returned and beckoned him through the door leading out the other side of the antechamber, away from the lobby. He stepped into the Council's main chamber and blinked in the bright light.

The council was assembled in two staggered semicircles of six large, darkened wood chairs, with a long bench running in front of them. A single seat was curiously empty. Sunlight streamed into the circular chamber through what appeared to be no ceiling at all, though Beddigan was sure some enchantment was in place to keep debris and rain from falling inside.

All eleven of the council members nodded as he approached

and stood on a square of red carpet trimmed with gold fillagree near the center of the room.

A very old Badger with a wispy white beard that he recognized from a job long ago, squinted at him from the far-right edge of the first row of council seats, "Ahh, welcome Beddigan T. Mouze. Your haste in responding to our summons is greatly appreciated."

Beddigan bowed deeply, "You are most welcome, Councilman Elgress."

The Badger swept a bony arm towards his compatriots, "I would introduce the council but the state is dire, and we cannot spare the time. You will have no doubt noticed that one member is vacant from this meeting?" Beddigan nodded, surveying the council, as Elgress continued, "We last saw our Councilman Anders from the Snowcap Mountains a week ago. He has always been aloof but when he did not show up to a council gathering, we began to worry something had happened. A few days later we received this." The Badger's shaking paw held up a sheet of parchment.

Beddigan stepped forward and retrieved it, reading quickly: it was a ransom letter. "He's been kidnapped," Beddigan mused aloud, rereading the letter. Elgress nodded. Beddigan continued, "Do you have any idea who is responsible?"

Elgress shook his head but gestured to a Bear who sat on the upper level of the council near the center, "As I mentioned, he was aloof and did not partake much in social activities. Björn here was closest to him, though he too has no idea why Anders was targeted or who may be responsible."

Beddigan noticed a slight shift in the Bear Councilman's eyes as Elgress continued to chatter on about the council's lack of suspects. Noting this, he returned his attention to Elgress, "May I have access to his chambers? I would like to see if he left us any clues."

Elgress was nodding his agreement when another council member, a Badger sow of middle years scoffed, "This is highly irregular, even for you, Elgress! This is a council problem, and the council should oversee the handling of it. I know you have worked with this *Mouse* before, but most of us have no reason to trust him."

Beddigan fixed his gaze on her sneering face, "I promise, madam, I am here only to help."

The Badger sow continued to sneer at him, "And collect your coin, eh? That is what you Adventurers do best."

Before Beddigan could respond, the Bear, Björn, spoke, his low voice barely more than a growl, "She has a point, Elgress. And outside access to a council members chamber is strictly forbidden." Beddigan's gaze sharpened on the Bear.

Elgress bashed his cane against the long bench, startling his fellow council members, "That is enough Councilwoman Everett! Now is not the time to raise disapproval at the decision to hire Beddigan. The majority voted for him and your cooperation is expected. And Councilman Björn, drastic times call for drastic measures." Turning his attention back to Beddigan, Elgress smiled, "Now then, if you will come with me I will show you to Anders quarters."

Beddigan nodded his goodbye to the rest of the council and followed Elgress out of the grand chamber. He slowed his pace and walked beside the old Badger as they made their way through the lobby, down a short hallway, and started up a spiral staircase. The second floor was where the missing Councilman's chambers were located.

Elgress stopped near the top of the staircase by an ornately carved door and fished inside his robes for a key ring. He selected a key and proceeded to unlock the door. The Badger gestured for Beddigan to enter, "I have been through the room myself and nothing stood out but then again I am much longer in my years than you."

Beddigan smiled at the old Badger, patting his shoulder as he slid past into the dark chamber. He pulled the heavy drapes open, bathing the room in sunlight. The bed was made up and the door to the adjoining washing room was pulled shut. A desk sat covered in folders and papers and a wardrobe sat ajar. A large chair sat near the doorway which Elgress proceeded to climb into to wait, as Beddigan searched.

Methodically he moved through the room, checking for signs of forced entry or struggle on the window frames, and around the door. He searched the wardrobe, finding only extra robes, clothing, and boots, as well as a small box of trinkets from his hometown. He dug through the papers on the desk, looking for anything that stood out, but not finding anything more than regular council business, just as Elgress had found.

Sitting on the edge of the bed facing Elgress, Beddigan eyed the Badger, "Unfortunately... nothing has jumped out at me as a clue to this mystery at all."

Elgress nodded, "I figured as much. This was as much a chance to be alone with you as it was an opportunity to get another set of eyes in here."

Beddigan smiled at the Councilman, "I too wished to ask you a few questions in private, old friend." Elgress nodded and Beddigan continued, "I noticed that of all the council members,

Councilman Björn seemed the least agreeable about my access to these chambers."

Elgress snorted, "Björn has always been a stickler for the rules; that Sinerrahan upbringing, you know." Beddigan agreed with a knowing grin, thinking about William. Elgress spoke again, "It's Councilwoman Everett that I am concerned is mixed up in this disappearance. She is the most confrontational and stubborn sow I have ever met! And she objected the most strongly to involving you in this."

Beddigan let that sink in, thinking about the previous encounter and the sow's obvious dislike of him. Standing up from the bed he spoke, "Well, I would like to speak with them both then."

With that, they left Anders' quarters and went in search of the other council members. Elgress led them to another hallway on the main level that had closed doors along it with each council member's name embossed on a brass plaque. First, they came to Councilwoman Everett's door, which remained solid and closed when they knocked.

Huffing, Elgress shuffled down the hall and knocked on the door with Councilman Björn's name only to receive the same stillness and quiet. They were about to turn away when a gruff voice behind them interrupted, "Looking for me?" the Bear questioned, looming tall over Elgress' small frame.

"A yes, Björn," Elgress said, "Beddigan would like a moment of your time." They stood aside as Björn moved into his office chambers, taking a seat behind a big, black desk.

Elgress gestured for Beddigan to follow the Bear inside, "I'll leave you to it then," the older Badger said as he turned away, closing the door behind him.

Beddigan sat in a similarly red covered chair to the one he had sat on in the antechamber earlier that day, and looked at the Bear across the desk, "Being that you were the closest to our missing Councilman, I was wondering if you might answer a few questions that I have?" The Bear nodded, gesturing for him to go on. "Was Anders having any issues in his home village that could have resulted in someone wanting to remove him from the Council?"

Björn thought a moment before answering, "Not that I am aware of."

Beddigan watched the Bear closely for signs of deceit, "So... his constituents were happy with his representation?"

The Bear nodded, "To my knowledge, yes."

Beddigan nodded along seeing no signs that the Bear was telling anything but the truth. "Did he ever mention anything to you about enemies, new or old? Or anyone who may be out to get him?"

The Bear's eyes shifted away for a moment, and the hesitation was clear. "Nothing I ever took seriously. He was a very paranoid Badger. Isolation can do strange things to a person, and he was alone up there in the mountains for a long time before he moved to the village he now represents."

Beddigan sensed something more was there but chose not to push. "Can you remember anything specific he may have mentioned that could assist me in finding him?"

The Bear watched him closely from across the desk, "How do I know his best interests are what you are after, Mouse?"

Beddigan groaned, scrubbing a paw over his face, "I get paid to do a job, much like you do, Councilman. My best interests are returning your missing council member unharmed and without having to fork over a huge amount of coin from your treasury. I am not here to trick you. I need as much information as you have if I am to rescue this compatriot of yours."

The Bear sat silently in response. Beddigan made another frustrated sound and stood to leave, but the Bear stopped him, "Wait," Björn hastened. Beddigan stopped near the door and turned back towards the Bear, waiting for him to continue. "He talked about 'snapping Wolves at his doorstep' often, but I always took it as an idiom. Perhaps he was referring to Mormant. There is a gang, here in the city, with strong ties to that land that I know he had some minor trouble with them in the past." Beddigan listened as Björn went on to explain how to find the gang. "That is all I know," the Bear finished.

Beddigan thanked him and left the Bear in his office chambers. His mind turned over the information slowly in his mind as he moved back to the lobby.

His steps hitched as he passed Councilwoman Everett's chambers, hearing muffled angry voices inside. He raised his paw to knock when the door flew open and another council member who he had not been introduced to flew past him, eyes sharp and paws clenched.

He peered in to see the Councilwoman angrily scrawling something on a piece of parchment. He cleared his throat, and she looked up, her face a mask of hostility. "What do you want, *Mouse*?" she snarled.

Beddigan stepped into the office, "I had a few questions about Councilman Anders disappearance."

With a scoff, she stood from her desk, stuffing the papers into her robes, "I don't have time for your questions. I am very busy. We are paying, a hefty sum I might add, to resolve this quickly and efficiently, so just get it on with it already." With that she breezed past him and out into the lobby.

Beddigan peered around her office for a moment, considering searching it, but instead left, pulling the door shut behind him. Despite his distrust of her, she was a council member, and he didn't really want her as any more of an enemy that she was already identifying herself to be.

He made his way out of the Council House and back into the sunny marketplace. He had some time to kill before nightfall when he could find and question a member of the gang Björn had told him about. He snagged an apple from a fruit stall and fished a coin out from his purse to give to the pretty young Badger sow manning the cart.

Walking along and munching on the apple he began to think about what a Councilman from the north would need from a gang with ties to Mormant, and what this ransom could be about. *Does it go all the way back to Mormant?* he thought. *Could there have been some trade deal with his village in the mountains?* he wondered.

And then it hit him: the realization almost caused him to choke on the bite of apple he had been chewing. "The land-bridge!" He gasped, dropping the apple core to the ground.

***

Beddigan leaned against the hard chairback, sipping his ale and surveying the dimly lit alehouse. It was not overly crowded, which was normal for a meeting place such as this, a common place for all manner of delinquents, thieves, and criminals.

He had chosen a little table near the back corner to wait for his guest to arrive. He had come early in the day to survey the establishment and speak with the owner. After paying a handsome fee, the owner had agreed to set up a meeting with a member of the gang that Councilman Björn had mentioned may know something of Councilman Anders' disappearance.

The door swung inward and a short, squat Badger shuffled in, eyes darting around the room. His gaze lingered on Beddigan for a moment before flickering away. He made his way to the bar and squawked his order for the cheapest ale to the owner. Once he had received his heavy pewter mug filled with frothy amber liquid, he shuffled around tables until he reached where Beddigan sat, "Yer Beddigan, yeah?" the Badger questioned, eyes narrowing as he looked Beddigan over.

Beddigan nodded, "And you are?" he questioned the Badger.

The Badger scowled, "Don't see whys you need my name."

Beddigan shrugged, "Alright, we can leave your name out of it. I am looking for information about a missing Councilman; his name is Anders and he's from the north."

The heavy mug slipped from the Badger's paw, thunking heavily on the worn and scratched wooden tabletop; ale sloshing over the rim. The Badger's eyes were wild and Beddigan was almost certain he was going to flee. Hastily, he held up his paws in a plaintive gesture, "No need to panic. I am not here to dig deep into your gang's affairs. I just need to find and return this missing Councilman," he said, attempting to sooth his guest.

The Badger stared at him for a long moment, before he picked up the mug and took a swig, paws still shaking, "I wouldn't know nothin' 'bout that," said the Badger, voice a bit hoarser than before.

Beddigan crossed his arms over his chest and cocked an

eyebrow, "Well now, isn't that just a shame?" he unhooked a small bag from his belt and dropped it on the table, the telltale sound of coins clinking together ringing out in the quiet room. "See, this bag of gold is earmarked for anyone who could help me. Now, are you certain you don't know anything about a missing Councilman?" He watched the Badger's beady eyes slide to the bag on the table. *Hook, line, and sinker*, Beddigan thought, fighting the urge to smile. Criminals and ruffians were easily persuaded.

"Maybe I's too hasty before," the Badger ventured, "I be knowin' somethin' of that after all." Beddigan pushed the bag of coins across the table and listened as the Badger launched into a detailed account of how the leader of his gang had abducted the Councilman and sent out the ransom letter. Beddigan listened, his brow furrowing deeper as the story went on.

Once the Badger had finished and was sipping from his mug of ale again, Beddigan spoke, "I see. Thank you for sharing those details with me. Do you know why Councilman Anders was targeted? Or where he is being held?" The Badger froze for an instant, barely noticeable to most, but Beddigan caught the falter in his gesture.

The Badger's eyes flickered up to meet his own, "He's at our Den, all safe an cozy like."

Beddigan nodded, "And as for why he was targeted?" The Badger averted his gaze, busying himself with counting the coins in the bag. Beddigan sighed, leaning back in his chair, "Look, I know your gang has ties to Mormant, and a fellow council member has expressed concern that Councilman Anders disappearance was somehow linked to that. Now, you clearly know more that you've shared and I am getting tired of this game. What will it take to get the whole truth out of you?"

Beddigan anticipated the greed before it was even reflected in the Badger's eyes.

"Dangerous ta share such information. I'd be requirin' a great deal more than's in this bag."

Beddigan loosened another bag of coins from his belt and held it up for the Badger to see. His new friend reached across the table greedily. Beddigan pulled the bag back out of reach, "Nuh uh," he tutted, "Information first, coin after."

The Badger snarled and settled back in his chair, "This Councilman of yours, ain't the kind of Badger you should be so concerned with savin'," the Badger paused to take a swig of ale. "He's a traitor an a dangerous one at that." Beddigan's heart sunk. *I knew it*, he thought. The area that Councilman Anders represented was the entirety of the Snowcap mountains and the foothills surrounding the frosty peaks, as well as the northern coastal section of Katheyra. The landbridge that ran between the continents, from Mormant to northern Katheyra, was nearly impassable even in the warmest part of the year. Few had dared venture across it and lived to tell the tale; only the most desperate chose that option, as sea travel and passage aboard a ship was costly.

Beddigan knew all too well how difficult it was to traverse the narrow, steep, and winding track. It took days to travel across with no break from the wind and frigid northern waters; no place to take shelter or camp. The closer one got to the Katheyran coast, the harder the trek became. For as long as anyone knew, a great gate had stood at the end of the bridge, barring anyone who had crossed from entering Katheyra. It had been several turnings since the gate had been manned by

Katheyran guards and stood still and locked at all times now.

When Beddigan had fled Mormant, he had done so by way of the landbridge; one of the lucky few to have crossed and lived. He knew from his time as a member of Her Majesty's Royal Sapphire Brigade, that in Mormant, themilitary had been trying to figure a way to exploit the landbridge as a weak point for an invasion of Katheyra for many turnings. While they had tried long ago to colonize Katheyra by naval ship, they had been met with the Republic's own naval forces and suffered a great defeat. The Council had always put Katheyra's freedom as its highest priority, and being a much larger country than Mormant, had rebuffed its attempts at war handsomely. The landbridge, however, was not monitored or manned any longer. Katheyra would be weak to an attack from the north, having most of their population in the central and southern parts of the land; even more so if it were a surprise attack.

The Badger continued, "Our leader, err, old leader, rest his soul, was helpin' ta facilitate a deal with this Councilman and General Hollister of Mormant for access through da landbridge gate."

Beddigan blew out a deep breath, "The fool!" he whispered harshly.

The Badger nodded eagerly, "Lotsa us in the gang didn't approve. I mean, imagine what would happen if Mormant took over everything here? No more gangs ta be sure."

Beddigan nodded, "So, what happened then? Why take Anders hostage if you were working with him?"

The Badger was signaling for another mug of ale and when he turned back, Beddigan was surprised to see sorrow in his beady eyes.

"As I said, we have a'new leader now. Our old leader weren't listenin' to our protests about not wantin' to get involved with Mormant in dis way. New leader took the old leader out an' took over. His idea to ransom the Councilman was met wit better favour."

Beddigan blew out another breath, more relief than wonder this time. He slid the second bag of coins over the tabletop, directly into the greedy little Badger's paw.

**

After getting the address of the gang's Den, and information on the best time to try and sneak the Councilman out from his well-paid new friend, Beddigan set about planning. The nameless Badger had informed him that their prisoner was being held in the back storage-room of the Den. Apparently there would only be one guard posted outside at night, as this was a brand-new Den and few knew of it.

He crept through the night, slinking from shadow to shadow in the alleys that ran behind the ramshackle houses in the poorer and rougher eastern quarter. He quickly located the Den and surveyed it from the back. It was dark and quiet, just as his informant had promised. There was a door at the back that hung askew on its hinges. According to the information he had received, it should be a simple job to slip in that door, and hang a right, knock out the guard, and rescue Councilman Anders.

Approaching carefully, one paw on the hilt of his sword, he pulled on the door's handle, wincing at the low groan of the un-greased hinges. He froze, waiting to see if any movement would follow at the sound. When no one came to investigate he slipped in the door and peered around the corner. Slumped on a stool, the guard was dozing next to a single door. *That must be the storage room*, he thought as he moved slowly towards the guard, who stank strongly of ale and snorted in his sleep.

Beddigan slipped his lock-picks out of a pouch on his belt and went about unlocking the door. Though he could see the keys hanging from a ring on the sleeping guards' belt, he thought it easier to let the drunkard sleep instead of creating a commotion by having to knock him out. The door clicked open and Beddigan waited a moment to see if the guard would rouse before he slipped inside. The room had no windows, and darkness blanketed it fully.

"Councilman?" he whispered as softly as he could. A grunt sounded from just to his right and he knelt down. Groping in the darkness, he had taken the lump for a sack of potatoes, and he had completely missed his mark, who was gagged with a dirty piece of fabric. Beddigan held a claw to his mouth to indicate that they must be quiet, hoping the Councilman's eyes had adjusted to the dark enough to see. He helped the Badger up by the arm, and carried him out of the room, tiptoeing out of the Den and back out into the still night.

Once they were a safe distance away down the alley, Beddigan untied the Councilman's paws and gag. He handed the Councilman his water skin and waited for the Badger to finish drinking and clearing his throat.

"T-thank you," the Badger finally managed, throat hoarse from disuse.

Beddigan handed the Councilman his own cloak for coverage and advised him to put the hood up for their journey back to the Council House, lest one of the gang members see and recognize him.

They made their way as quickly as they could through the streets, and Anders squeaked happily when the sight of his workplace and residence came into view. The night steward greeted them at the doors, rushing forward eagerly to allow Anders to return home.

"Please alert all members of the Council of his return immediately. We will be waiting in the Council's main chamber." The steward nodded and scurried off to do Beddigan's bidding.

"Oh b-but I wish only to return to my chambers," Councilman Anders shaking voice argued.

Beddigan fixed the Badger in his gaze, disapproval radiating from him, "I think your fellow council members deserve to know the truth of your disappearance, Councilman Anders. Treachery is not a thing to save until morning." He then gripped the slight Badger's elbow firmly and pushed him through the lobby toward the main chamber's doors.

"Unhand m-me!" the Badger yelped, trying to shake loose of Beddigan's tight grip.

Beddigan rounded on him with a snarl, "Do not test me, Councilman. I am not above binding you up like I found you. You deserve far worse!" he spat, shoving the Badger through the big, swinging doors that lead into the main chambers. Dragging a chair from the edge of the room next to the petitioner's circle, he ordered the Councilman to sit while they waited.

Soon the other council members were filtering through the doors, in various stages of dress and alertness.

Councilwoman Everett sneered at him, "Guess you *can* do some things right." Beddigan gave her a frosty look, turning away to greet Elgress as he entered last, shuffling forward to greet Beddigan and welcome Anders home. Beddigan cast his gaze over the assembled council members, noting the various levels of confusion, especially those that had clearly noted the pained look and nervous nature of their returned member.

Elgress took his seat at the council Elder's bench, "Welcome home Anders and thank you very much, Beddigan, our saviour!" The old Badger beamed from beneath tufted white brows. Beddigan bowed graciously to the elder, thanking him for his kind words, and then moved to address the group.

"I suppose you're all wondering why I have called you here at such a late hour, when a simple message of Anders return would have sufficed." Several of the council members nodded.

Councilwoman Everett lounged back in her seat, a look of annoyance plastered on her face, "You best have a good reason, Mouse," she scoffed.

Elgress shot her a frustrated look, but Beddigan held up a paw to stop any censure the old Badger may have been planning on hurling at the Councilwoman.

"A very good reason, indeed, Councilwoman Everett. The reason I called this assembly is the same reason Anders sits here and not among you. He is a traitor." The room erupted with rumblings at Beddigan's blunt statement. He held up his paw again, in an attempt to quiet the room enough to continue. Once the murmurs had diminished, he explained briefly about Anders' transgressions, keeping a firm grip on the Councilman's shoulder.

Several members of the council gasped at the revelations. Björn spoke first, "Anders, you fool!" the Bear snarled, his fist coming down on the bench with barely restrained fury, "You seek to sell us out to those Wolves for what? What could they have possibly offered you that was enough to turn your back on us all?"

Anders' head had been hung low through Beddigan's explanation. He raised it slowly, looking up at the council with sorrow reflected on his face, "Freedom," he whispered.

Björn made a frustrated sound and leaned back in his chair. Elgress spoke next, "Anders, you were protected here. Safe. What freedom is it... what is so important to you?"

Anders sobbed, head falling to his paws, "You've no idea what it is like having the Wolves at your heels. Always."

Björn stood again with a frustrated growl, "And whose fault was it that they were after you, Anders? Yours alone. You got in bed with them long ago. It is our mistake that we believed those ties were severed."

Councilwoman Everett stood up, "Now just a moment here, am I missing something? Since when did Anders have any sort of relationship with Mormant? Why was he allowed to run for council with that history?" She looked pointedly at Elgress, "Another one of your dreadful mistakes, I assume?" she sneered.

Elgress stood and moved from his seat down to the floor of the council chamber and moved to stand next to Beddigan, "While I do not take responsibility for Anders' transgressions, I did play a part in this by accepting his candidacy despite his past. For this, I am sorry. Björn, please arrange for the guards to pick Anders up. The rest of you are dismissed for the night. We can address any questions or concerns you may have in the morning."

The council members murmured to each other as they filed out of the room. Björn disappeared through a different door to a different wing of the Council House and returned with two guards. They proceeded to remove the still sobbing Anders without any further conversation.

Björn approached Beddigan, holding out his paw. Beddigan gripped it and accepted the Bear's thanks. Björn then left, leaving Elgress and Beddigan alone in the large, empty room.

"You can pick up your fee at the front desk on your way out. Thank you, Beddigan. Thank Annalose and Ardra that even our city's gangs relish the freedom we seek to provide for all Katheyran's." Beddigan nodded, falling into step beside the old Badger as they slowly made their way out to the lobby.

"What will happen now?" he asked, pausing as the elderly Badger stopped to adjust his robes.

"Well, Anders will be removed from his seat and we will elect a new representative from the Snowcap region as soon as possible." They resumed walking, and Elgress continued, "This was close though. Too close. I will be stepping down as Council Elder immediately, so the council will be quite busy finding my replacement for my constituency, as well as electing a new leader internally."

Beddigan placed a paw on his old friend's back, "I'm sorry to hear that Elgress. You were a great council member and an even better leader."

Elgress smiled graciously, "Thank you, Beddigan. But my time is done in that role. I think it has been for a while now."

Beddigan nodded and wished his friend a fond farewell as the older Badger shuffled down the hallway towards the stairs that would lead up to his chambers.

"You never know, retirement may suit you." Beddigan called after him.

Elgress turned slowly, his eyes twinkling, "We'll see if you ever think that for yourself, Beddigan." And with that Elgress disappeared around the corner, his soft chuckles echoing through the lobby.

Chapter 9: She Ain't Seaworthy

Beddigan sat down on the edge of the quiet dock, swinging his legs over the edge, skimming the bottom of his bare feet over the clear water. His boots sat next to him, freshly cleaned and oiled, gleaming mahogany in the bright sunshine. Aside from the empty dock he sat on, the marina was a flurry of activity. The shade from the city's outer wall fell just short of where he sat. The western gate of the city of San Vincent's Port was split into two sections: to the north was the visitor and merchant gate, dubbed The West Gate, and to the south was the port-marina gate, for all sea travellers and traveling merchants, known as the Sea Traveller's Gate.

Shading the sun from his eyes Beddigan scanned the boats and tall ships for what felt like the millionth time, looking for the familiar flag of one Captain Linley. He was almost certain that the Fillsner's Muse, the ship he had ridden upon to visit William's wife, and many times prior to that, was not docked in the marina, which befuddled him as he had received word that Captain Linley had arrived in the city. There had been instructions to meet the captain that morning, yet he had seen no sign of the peculiar little Badger, his ship, or any of his familiar crew. On top of this disturbing circumstance, William, who had been traveling to meet him to join this new quest had been delayed, though he too should be arriving that day. He only hoped William would show up in time to set sail, that is, if he could ever find the damn ship he was supposed to be on.

The two Adventurers had signed on for what would likely be a most interesting journey: the first expedition to the Ranier Islands either of them had heard of in many turnings. Many explorers had tried to sail to the Islands in turnings past, and never returned, or had returned empty handed, with tales of a mist that could not be penetrated. Most had never even seen the mist that hung as a veil between the Islands and the Lorring Sea. Even fewer had glimpsed the clusters of Islands barely visible beyond it.

Had it been any other captain, requesting them as part of the crew, they would have given a resounding and heartfelt decline in response, but Captain Linley was not only a fine ship captain, but he was also no fool. Though the Badger hadn't revealed many details in the request for Beddigan to join his crew for the journey, he felt the lingering promise that some new information had been discovered by the wily Badger; some key to unlock the secrets of those Islands.

And after his recent encounters with both Shianne and the Lynx Sorceress, he was most excited to see what all this could lead to.

A shadow fell over Beddigan from the back, and a huge paw came down on his shoulder. He turned to see a familiar face, "You finally made it," Beddigan said with a crooked smile, looking up into his good friend William's face.

The Bear chuckled, "You know as well as any that a trip never goes exactly to plan."

Beddigan nodded his agreement, standing up and using a rag from his bag to dry his feet. He pulled on his boots and stood, embracing his friend in a quick, short hug. "Well, now that you're here, all we need to do is find Captain Linley and set off."

William's brow furrowed, "Find him?" the Bear questioned.

Beddigan sighed and surveyed the ships one more time, "Word came of his arrival but his ship is nowhere to be seen. I thought maybe he had gotten a new ship, but I haven't seen his flag flying either."

As if on cue, two Badgers, dressed in swabby gear, veered off of the path leading from the Sea Traveller's Gate, "Aye, Beddigan? William?" the taller of the two squawked. Beddigan nodded. The Badgers gestured for them to follow and headed down the length of the marina. Beddigan and William fell into step behind them as they passed ship after ship.

As they got closer to the north end of the marina, Beddigan's brow began to furrow. When the Badgers stopped at the final ship moored along the strip, his heart sank. The ship was much smaller than a typical tall ship, and shabbier as well. It had seen some rough sea travel in its day.

William leaned down towards him, "Is this thing even seaworthy?" the Bear murmured incredulously. Beddigan shrugged and shot William a worried look, as they followed the Badgers up the gangway.

Once aboard the ship, Beddigan was even more disappointed in its failing structure. As they followed the Badgers to back of the ship, and up the steps to the wheel where Captain Linley would likely be found, they had to pick their way around actual holes in the floorboards of the deck.

"Watch yer step!" their escort added as William nearly tripped and fell into a barely covered hole.

William growled, "What kind of joke is this?" the Bear snarled, as they departed from their escort and started up the steps to the back of the ship. The steps groaned under the weight of the heavy Bear.

Beddigan was relieved to see Captain Linley exactly as he remembered. The squat little Badger wore a huge captain's hat, nearly double the width of his body. Standing atop a crate by the ship's wheel, he was barking orders to people on the deck below.

"Patchers, you need to do a better job than that if she's to be seaworthy again. And hurry! At the rate y'all be working we won't be sailing for another turning." Captain Linley caught sight of them and turned, grinning at Beddigan as he approached, "Ahh, you've arrived! Yes! Hello Beddigan, a right pleasure to see you again."

Beddigan greeted the captain and shook his paw. Gesturing to William he introduced the Bear, "Captain Linley, this is my associate William, the one who agreed to sign on for this mission with me. William, this is the infamous Captain Linley."

Linley's eyes bugged out a bit as he peered up at the towering Bear.

William extended his paw and gingerly shook the captains still outstretched one, "A pleasure to meet you, Captain," the Bear mumbled.

Linley blinked, "A yes — yes, you too William! You too." He leapt down from the crate and shuffled past them, beckoning them to follow him. He led them around the ship in a makeshift tour, though huge parts of the vessel went unexplored as they were under repairs at the moment.

Once they had returned full circle to the wheel Beddigan

asked, "Forgive me, Captain, but what happened to the Fillsner's Muse?"

Linley groaned and leaned against the crate with a sigh, "Ahh, Beddigan, this journey is proving to be a bit of a bear," he shot William a quick glance, adding, "No offence."

William's voice was a rumble over the hustle and bustle going on around them on the ship, "None taken."

Linley hastily returned his gaze to Beddigan, "As you can imagine, getting information about how to get to the Ranier Islands has been most difficult. I have spent my life collecting tidbits here and there, in hopes of being the first in generations to sail through those mists and return to speak of it. A break in the case came a few weeks ago, which was when I summoned you, and asked for your assistance on this journey." He scrubbed a paw over his face, sighing, "The information turned out to be incomplete. We need to retrieve something before we can sail, and due to financial circumstance, I had to sell the Fillsner's Muse to buy these," he added, pulling out two large, bright purple crystals from a pouch on his belt.

Beddigan recognized them immediately, "A portal?" he questioned.

Linley nodded, admiring the crystals for a moment, "Yes, Beddigan. What we need is located in Ashra's Point, and we haven't the time to travel there across land to get it. Damn that Warbler's Cursed east side of Katheyra!" Linley snarled, thumping his little fist against the crate

Beddigan stifled a chuckle at the little Badger's display of anger. "So, I take it you would like William and I to travel to Ashra's Point using these portal crystals, retrieve this item, and then return to begin the journey?" Beddigan asked.

Linley nodded, rattling off the details of who to contact, and where in Ashra's Point they could be found. "We will continue trying to make this scrap heap sea-worthy in your absence. She's all I could afford after sending payment for the item you are picking up and buying these portals." The captain placed the crystals into Beddigan's paw. "Now off with you! And hurry back." He squawked, shuffling off to bark more orders at his crew.

Beddigan looked up at William, "Perhaps you should draw the portal, being so much taller than I," Beddigan said, with a grin. William snatched one of the crystals from his paw. Beddigan watched him close his eyes, picturing Ashra's Point before he drew a sweeping oval in the air with the crystal. The air distorted inside the shimmering purple circle, and when he was finished, the crystal had faded from bright purple to a dull grey.

He followed William through the portal. It snapped shut behind them, with a delicate *pop* and a rush of air. Beddigan's breath caught in his throat. It always took the wind from his lungs whenever he traveled by portal. His body knew it was unnatural and let him know it handsomely.

William shuddered, "It always gives me the heebie-jeebies going through those things," the Bear grumbled.

Beddigan nodded and surveyed their surroundings. They had appeared on a path just outside of a thick cropping of trees. The path lead in a winding track down the slope to the small village of Ashra's Point, perched on the rocky cliffs overlooking the Trelill Sea. It always astonished him how different the water looked from the Lorring Sea, to which he was accustomed. Instead of deep, dark blues of the western sea, this expanse of water was tinted a stunning aquamarine. It stretched out to the horizon, getting lighter as it went. He stared at it the whole way down the pathway until they reached the village, and the ocean dropped below his sightline.

Following Captain Linley's instructions, they moved through the quiet village, nodding to the villagers and merchants they passed, who watched them with curious looks. Not many travellers found their way to this village, with no major roadways leading to or from it, and with the east coast of Katheyra being so sparsely populated, it wasn't a surprise that the villagers were interested in them. Reaching the far edge of the village they followed a winding path east, climbing along rocky terrain until they reached another outcropping of trees. They walked silently through the rustling evergreens until they reached a fork, slighting right towards the coastline. They emerged from the forest into a clearing with a large cottage perched close to the edge of the cliffs; cliffs that dropped straight down to the aquamarine water below.

"Pretty far out of the village to be living," William commented, as they approached the cottage.

Beddigan shrugged, "If you collected antiquities and magical items, wouldn't you want to be tucked away somewhere?"

William shrugged as they came to a stop in front of the cottage door.

Beddigan raised his paw to knock when a squeaky voice called out through the un-shuttered window, "It's open!"

Beddigan's paw froze, and hung in the air a moment before he registered the voice, and turned the knob, entering the cottage. The cottage was larger than average, but horribly cluttered. There were stacks of books, boxes, and crates nearly to the roof in every part of every room. Some rustling to the right drew their attention.

"Hello?" Beddigan called out.

A small, graying Badger rustled out from under a table; the size of a child but with many years to his name. He greeted Beddigan by clasping both his dusty paws over Beddigan's, "Ah yes yes yes yes *yes*! You must be the buyer! Captain something or somesuch?" the little Badger said with a gap-toothed grin, spectacles perched low on his nose, dust clumps stuck to his whiskers. His beady little eyes looked past Beddigan to William, "My word!" he squeaked, "Well aren't you just a big one then, hmm?" The little Badger said with a chuckle, zipping past them and rummaging through boxes.

Beddigan met William's eyes and shrugged, his eyes dancing with laughter, "Sorry to disappoint," Beddigan said, "But I am not actually Captain Linley. He merely sent me to pick up the item that you have sold him."

The little Badger looked up from the crate he was digging in and frowned, "A pity. I do so like meeting the buyers of my merchandise," he said, pushing the crate aside to get to another crate. He popped the top off of it and dug around with one paw, until his face lit up and he yanked a cloth wrapped bundle from the wooden box. "Ahh, yes! Yes yes yes yes *yes*!" he squeaked triumphantly, holding up the bundle for them to see. Beddigan and William exchanged a look. The little Badger rustled over to a table in the corner, one of the only surfaces in the cottage without things piled on top of it. "Come come *come* see! Yes yes yes yes *yes*!" he squeaked excitedly again, carefully unwrapping the bundle from its cloth.

Beddigan peered down and let out a soft gasp. There on the table, in a pool of white linen sat the largest and most perfectly oval crystal he had ever seen. It shimmered, iridescently, looking a different sparkling colour from each direction. It was encased in a gold capsule; a frame of some sort, that was tarnished with thick black smudges of grease. The little Badger grabbed the edge of the linen it had been wrapped in and started busily rubbing the grease free from the casing.

"I've never seen anything like it," William murmured.

Beddigan nodded and the little Badger turned around, giving them a cross look, "Well, of course you haven't," he snapped, "My collection is the single greatest in all of Katheyra. And no one has seen or used a crystal such as this in ages. *Ages!*" His beady little eyes sparkled with barely restrained excitement. "Yes yes yes yes *yes*! Hard to let go this treasure was, but things are meant to be used! They can't all stay with me forever," he babbled, no longer even looking at Beddigan or William. Beddigan held in his laughter and gingerly wrapped the crystal in the cloth it had originally been wrapped in as the Badger flitted off to dig through more crates.

William had already left the cottage. Beddigan peered around, looking for the peculiar old Badger but all he could see was stacks of things. He could hear rustling but couldn't tell where it was coming from.

"Thank you!" he called, leaving the cottage and pulling the door shut behind him.

William rolled his eyes and Beddigan finally let loose the chuckles he had been holding in as they made their way up the path and out of earshot, "What a crackpot," William said, laughter gilding in his voice.

Beddigan fished the other portal crystal out of his crystals pouch and handed it to William, "Quite the character," he mused, as William drew the portal.

They stepped through, both shivering at the peculiar sensation again, and found themselves near the city wall by the Sea Traveller's Gate. They laughed the whole way down the path to the marina and were still chuckling about the crazy old Badger when they reached the gangway to the shabby ship of Captain Linley's.

Though they hadn't been gone long, Beddigan was pleased with how the repairs were coming, and was happy to see they had hoisted Linley's flag. Asking a crew member for the captain's whereabouts, they were ushered below decks to the captain's cabin. Pushing open the door, Beddigan winced, having to duck low.

Poor William, he thought as he heard the Bear grunt to shrink down enough to enter the small room. Captain Linley sat behind his desk pouring over maps, and looked up with excitement when he heard them enter.

"Good lads, you've got it, have you?" Linley said, scrubbing his paws together eagerly.

Beddigan struggled to remove the bundle from his bag in the small quarters, but got it free and set it on Linley's desk, "We did, indeed. Now, what exactly is it that we have just retrieved for you?" He asked curiously. He felt William crowd close as Linley unveiled the shimmering crystal again, to get a look at the marvelous thing.

Running his paw over the smooth finish of the gem, Linley looked up at Beddigan and William and said, glee filling his eyes, "This, my friends, is the key to penetrating the mists of the Ranier Island."

***

Beddigan watched the eerie green-gray mists of the Rainier Islands grow ever closer, as the ship sailed over the choppy Lorring Sea. Having never sailed this close to them before, they were all surprised by the greenish tint to the mists, which had always appeared more like a gray-white fog from a distance. The closer they got to the mists, the more details they could see beyond them. From a distance, the mists looked as if they shifted and blew, akin to sea spray, but as they got closer to the phenomenon, it almost looked as if the mists were frozen into a shield of sorts; like a green-hued frost blooming upon glass.

Captain Linley barked orders from the helm of the ship, slowing the vessel and angling their approach. One member of the small, skeleton crew was charged with making sure the gem was affixed to the bow of the ship securely. He held a rope that was attached to the gold casing of the crystal, which was nailed to the wood of the bow, just in case it should come loose. None of them knew what would happen when they reached the edge of the mists to breach them, or what would happen if they were to lose the gem partway through.

They were very close to the mists now and Captain Linley had slowed the ship further, trying for a careful approach, but the bucking and rolling of the waves beneath them made a stealthy approach difficult.

Beddigan hung his head over the railing of the deck, and William patted his back, "Try and focus on the excitement, friend."

Beddigan turned and gave the Bear a watery smile, feeling another wave of queasiness roll through him. *Why did I sign up for this, again?* he thought bitterly, standing and stretching, attempting to ease the tightness in his belly. His breath caught in his throat as they angled east, only a few yards away from their first attempt at penetrating the mists.

The green-grey mist loomed like a wall of frozen air in front of them.

Through it though, they could make out the dark, hulking shapes of the Islands themselves.

"Annalose and Ardra..." William breathed. None aboard had ever gotten close enough to see the actual Islands behind the mist.

"A marvel," Beddigan murmured as they headed to the back of the ship where Linley was squawking excitedly.

"Prepare yourselves to make history, lads!" Linley greeted them, his beady eyes sparkling like onyx.

William looks tense, Beddigan noted, as they took up a place beside the small Badger atop a crate behind the ship's big wheel. It wasn't surprising that William wasn't quite as excited as the captain or Beddigan himself. He had been skeptical of Linley's explanation for how this gem would work, as well as lacking confidence in the ship, the crew, and the lack of weapons aboard. Linley had argued that the crazy old Badger they had got the gem from in Ashra's Point had personally recovered it from a shipwreck many turnings ago that flew the Ranier Islands flag; or at least what they thought the flag was as it hadn't been seen in generations.

William had argued that anything that twitchy old coot had said should be taken with a grain of salt, and Beddigan partially agreed. However, here they were, aboard the ramshackle ship and about to breach the mists.

Beddigan's excitement was beginning to outweigh his nausea

as they drifted ever closer.

The bow of the ship came into contact with the wall of mist with an ear- piercing shriek. Beddigan fell hard to his knees, paws covering his ears as the breath was knocked from his lungs. By the time he returned to his feet, most of the crew had recovered.

Captain Linley still looked a bit dazed, "Wasn't expecting that," the captain grumbled.

William's face was twisted into a snarl, "So now, not only are we largely unarmed, but we basically rung the damn doorbell!" he growled.

Beddigan put a paw on his friend's shoulder, "Deep breaths, William. We don't know if that was something only we could hear or not. We know very little, so try and remain calm until there is a reason not to be."

William started to respond but stopped as a rush of cool air slid over the deck of the ship, and they realized they had successfully passed through the mists.

"Annalose alive... we've done it," Linley breathed, as the ship slid across the calm water towards a small cluster of islands.

The Ranier Islands rose from the water at high angles, covered with evergreen trees and various thick, heavy brush. Towering cliffs, sheer drops, and ragged coastlines ringed each of the islands that they could see. To the right, a much larger island rested.

Beddigan was staring at the islands at a loss for words when William called to him, "Beddigan, look!"

He whirled around to see the Bear at the back railing of the ship looking in the direction that they had come from. He gasped, astonished, as he saw the mists from the inside for the first time. Like diamonds shattered across black velvet, it was as if the night sky began at the water, stretching up, lightening as it went until it became the sunshine-filled, clear blue sky of the day outside the barrier. "Magnificent," he murmured, turning back to Linley who was already back to barking orders.

They were pulling the ship towards the right now, away from the small cluster of islands to the one larger island, where there was sandspit that they could moor along. Beddigan felt his gaze drawn back to the smaller cluster of islands though, catching sight of flashes of bright light and a moving, shimmering iridescence, like that of the gem that had allowed them access to this wondrous place.

How do you get to them? He wondered, eyeing the sheer cliffs rising up from the water. He tore his gaze away and fell in with the rest of the crew, getting the ship moored along the strip of sand.

Leaving the crew behind, Beddigan, Linley, and William disembarked and moved down the spit to the strip of beach that seemed to ring the island; at least what they could see of it, stretching around the natural curve of the land. William wore a grim frown as they forged ahead into the bush, navigating between trees until they found a worn, though overgrown pathway.

The foliage here looked familiar, for the most part. Conifers and ferns, moss, and shrubbery like those native to Sinerrah and Katheyra. But the further they moved inland, the more the surroundings changed.

Tall trees with reddened bark towered above them, with branches starting several yards above their heads. The bark cracked and peeled away from the trunk, revealing shiny purple insides. Shrubs with blue and pink leaves started to take over the more familiar plants, and fruit trees hung over the pathway, displaying their wares. Beddigan plucked a piece of fruit from a branch near his head and marveled at it: it looked like the typical red apples they had in Katheyra, though it was bright green. He sniffed it and smiled at the pleasant smell. Linley snatched it from his paw to inspect as they continued along the path.

A sudden crunch caused both Beddigan and William to look back, where they saw Linley munching the apple-like fruit.

William lurched forward, batting the partially eaten fruit from the little Badger's paw, "You fool, " the Bear hissed, "It could be poison!"

Linley shrugged at the Bear and continued down the path as if nothing had happened, "Tastes fine," the Badger murmured. Beddigan turned his head away to stifle his laughter, as his friend stared at the little Badger, mouth agape.

"Come along then lads, we have much to explore!" Linley called back to them as they approached a grove of trees that had white and dark blue striped bark. The leaves were such a dark blue they were nearly black, and clusters of yellow berries hung high in them.

Beddigan quickly ushered Linley through the grove before the Badger could try and find some more foreign snacks, and they were soon back along the densely forested path. It grew darker as the trees towered above them, and though they knew it should be daylight, it started to look like nighttime.

Orange light flickered in the distance and Beddigan held a claw to his mouth, signaling for quiet, and lead them aside into the brush as they approached the light. They neared the edge of the woods, crouching low behind shrubs with large, purple fruits, and peered into what looked like a very small, rustic village.

There was a large ring of what looked like dwellings, only made from cloth draped over a wooden structure. There were a couple of long banquet tables made from roughly-hewn wood, and a roaring fire in the center of the camp, which cast the flickering orange light that they had seen through the trees.

Beddigan's heart rate quickened as they observed beings in robes, moving to and from the banquet tables and around the fire. Hoods drawn up and with long, draping sleeves, it was impossible to tell if they were Lynx. The robes looked familiar though; very familiar, and William noticed this detail as well. Keeping his voice low, William murmured, "Sorcerers."

Beddigan nodded, and turned to the other two, "We best backtrack and avoid them if we plan to explore anything else," he whispered. Linley nodded in agreement, and they turned, trying not to rustle any bushes.

Beddigan gasped and his paw flew to the hilt of his sort when a voice sounded behind them, "You best come out now. We've known of your presence since you made landfall."

William drew his daggers with a snarl, whirling to face the voice, but he too gasped upon seeing their perceived enemy. Standing with its back to the roaring fire was one of the cloaked beings, though the hooded cloak it wore was silver instead of the black that the others were wearing. The hood was pulled back so that they could see the face of the creature within; with the height and stature of Bear, but with skin unlike anything he had seen before; delicate scales framed the face of the androgynous being.

"Please, join us travellers. We wish to ask you much," the

creature said in a lilting voice, gesturing for them to come out of the brush.

Shooting nervous glances at one another they followed the creature to the fireside. The other cloaked beings revealed similar features as their hoods were drawn back.

"What are you?" Linley blurted in amazement as his eyes travelled around the throng of beings, voicing Beddigan and William's thoughts.

Beddigan winced but waited as the silver-cloaked being spoke, "We are sorcerers, as I am sure you have guessed. And we are the original inhabitants of these lands."

Beddigan's mind reeled. The scales, he noticed, extended to the backs of the claws of the beings as well and he felt his blood chill. *They almost look like they are...* he thought, gasping before finishing the thought.

The eerie yellow eyes of the creature fastened on him and its mouth stretched wide, revealing sharp, jagged teeth. "Ah, this one has guessed it."

"Dragons..." Beddigan whispered.

William brandished his daggers again with a snarl, and Linley made a choking sound.

"Back, you devils!" William growled.

The being in the silver cloak chuckled, a hoarse sound, "Not Dragons as you know them. Be calm, Bear." The being spoke soothingly, "But related to them, yes," it continued.

Beddigan reached over and placed a paw on William's arm, silently urging him to put his weapons away. He eyed the being warily, "We encountered a sorceress... a Lynx, which we had believed inhabited these Islands. Though she could take other forms." Beddigan hesitated for a moment before continuing,

"Which of you is the *real* indigenous inhabitant of the Ranier Islands... is the question I am left with."

The being scowled, along with several of the others, "Long ago we gifted magic to this world, magic beyond the crystals like those hanging from your belt. Long before your kinds walked these lands and those beyond, we existed; lived, thrived. Once we began to share these lands with you all, we chose to share our gifts among you. The greediest received the least potential, in an effort towards balance. We began to be hunted by the avaricious, so we retreated here and put up our wall of mist. There were so few of us left."

The being shook his head in grief, "The Lynx people that lived here were unknown to us and the rest of the world, as sea travel had not yet come to pass. Savage and uncultured, we partnered with them for mutually beneficial ends. We gifted them with strong magic, and they cared for us, in our wounded and depleted state."

The being was pacing now, claws clasped behind their back as it told the painful story, "We existed like that for many turnings, as almost gods to the Lynx. But soon, their culture began to evolve. They wished to leave the safety of our Islands. We tried to stop them, but they turned on us, exiling us to this one island. We had created monsters, easily capable of wiping us out. And so, we have lived here, funneling a great deal of our power into the barrier so that we may be safe."

Beddigan was stunned. The information filtered into his brain, arranging itself as he tried to make sense of it.

"Have you no contact with the Lynx, then?" he asked, remembering the vicious nature of the sorceress who had plagued the village with ghosts of their loved ones.

The being shook its head, "None. We assume they have taken over the rest of the world. Their power is awesome; few could stand against it," the being mused.

Captain Linley was grinning excitedly, wrapped up in the narrative, "Oh no! But you see they have not been seen in generations! Most don't believe they even exist any longer."

The being looked at him sharply, "But what of the one you saw?" he questioned Beddigan.

Beddigan shrugged, "As I said, she could take other forms, so perhaps they move among the countries in disguise, but this was the first occurrence any of us had heard of, of actually seeing a Lynx."

The being started mumbled to the other beings in a language that they did not understand. William and Beddigan exchanged looks of bewilderment.

After some time, the being turned back to them, looking saddened and concerned, "You must go," it spoke, a group of the other beings falling into step while he ushered them onto the path that would lead back to the sandspit. "You must hurry. They will have been alerted to your presence as we were."

They rushed through the forest, wordless. They reached the strip of beach at a dead run, fear adding to their haste. Linley yelped up to ship, "Prepare to disembark! Quickly, lads, quickly!"

They turned to face the beings, and Beddigan reached out to clasp the arm of the one who had spoken with them, "We will return, when we are better prepared for a rescue mission." He said earnestly.

The being shook his head, "There is no place left for us in the world. You should never return here," he croaked.

Beddigan searched the Dragon-like face for a moment.

"Beddigan, come! We must go!" William called from the gangway. With one last squeeze of the being's arm, Beddigan released it and raced up to the ship.

The crew was heaving the sails and Linley was atop his crate, navigating and barking orders. They picked up speed, heading towards the night-sky looking barrier. Beddigan turned to the back of the ship and saw flashes of light coming from the beach. He gripped the railing and watched as several beings in bright blue robes cast balls of fire at the lone silver-cloaked creature.

"William, come! Look!" he yelped to his friend who raced over. They both doubled over, paws pressed to their ears as the ship's bow breached the barrier, causing another ear-piercing shriek. When they had recovered from it, they were in the mists. Beddigan strained to see the island, the flashes of light had stopped.

William leaned down, "Is it over? Was the creature killed?" the Bear asked.

Beddigan strained, trying to make sense of what he saw, which was a huge form on the beach, "By Annalose..." he whispered, realizing that in place of the creature which had been about William's size, was the still form of a huge, lumbering, silver Dragon. He turned to William, gripping a handful of the Bear's tunic, "Annalose and Ardra, William, those creatures were Dragon-born."

William shook loose of Beddigan's grip, as the ship popped free of the mists and back out onto the rolling Lorring Sea, "Dragon-born?"

Beddigan braced himself against the railing, breathing heavy, "Dragon's that can take animal-form, like that which we saw. Legend and myth. The most powerful of the Dragons. Some believe they birthed the Dragons we know of and loathe into the world. Others believe that Dragons created the Dragon-Born to rule the world in their stead."

William's eyes flew wide, and he shoved Beddigan to the ship's deck, "Get down!" he hollered, "They've come after us!"

Beddigan watched a ball of light whiz past where his head had been. He had been so distracted he hadn't even noticed a ship appearing behind them on the water, approaching quickly and armed with Lynx sorcerers in their flapping blue robes. Linley began barking orders at the crew, but Beddigan could feel it already, as the ship lurched and bucked, shivering as balls of blue fire hit the hull.

They were going down, and fast.

Crawling with William towards Linley, he breathed to his friend, "Thanks."

William growled in response, "Thank me when we make it through this alive," he said sourly.

Beddigan toppled and rolled across the deck, slamming hard into the railing as the boat lurched and started to sink.

"Abandon ship! Abandon ship!" Linley squawked.

William stood, trying to get his bearings, and Beddigan watched in horror as a ball of light slammed into the Bear's chest. He tried to scramble across the deck to reach his friend but fighting against the bucking of the boat was too much. He watched as William stumbled backwards; one step, two steps, finally toppling over the railing.

"William!" Beddigan yelled, "Bear overboard!" He scrambled across the deck, peering over the side to see if he could see William in the water below.

Several crew members had climbed into the lifeboats, along

with Linley. "Beddigan, get in the boat!" Linley yelled up to him, but he was still searching the water below. No sign of William.

Beddigan stood, turning to face the attackers with a snarl, and was shocked to see the boat had turned about and was retreating. He was suddenly aware of the flurry around him, as crew members abandoned the lifeboat that had made its way to water and started to sink immediately, having been damaged by the fight. The boat teetered as it took on water and Linley squawked orders for crew to bail and stay near the high parts. Hearing a shuddering creak, Beddigan turned, just in time to see part of the mast come crashing down. He stared as it swung towards him, unable to move.

***

Beddigan awoke with a shuddering gasp. His stomach rolled as he felt the bobbing and heaving of a ship's deck beneath him. He scrambled over onto his side, vomiting and coughing heavily.

A paw thumped against his back, "Ah, you're awake. Glad to see it," a familiar voice said.

Once his eyes had quit watering, he turned and looked up to see a Wolf in bright regalia, fitting of a ship's captain. His eyes focused and he recognized the Wolf with a rush of relief as Captain Marlog. Sitting up he cast his eyes around the deck, recognizing most of the crew and Captain Linley in similar positions on the deck; sitting, resting, or coughing up sea water.

Beddigan looked up at the captain, "Thank you. I'm not sure how you happened to rescue us all, but we owe you a great debt, indeed," he said, voice hoarse.

The Captain nodded, his face grim, "It is unfortunate that we could not save you all."

Beddigan felt his heart drop.

Linley waddled over, giant hat in paw, "Beddigan, I'm sorry," he murmured.

Beddigan nodded jerkily, accepting Linley's condolences.

As the Badger shuffled away to check on his crew, Marlog knelt next to him, "It was the oddest thing though," he murmured, "I saw your Bear floating on a chunk of wood, very much alive, as we approached for rescue. And then," the captain snapped his claws, "Just like that he disappeared."

Beddigan's eyes sharpened on the Wolf's face, "Disappeared, like got taken under by the water? Or disappeared, like vanished?" he questioned.

The Wolf's eyes sparkled with interest, "I had assumed he sunk, but something tells me that may not be the case."

Beddigan sucked in a sharp breath as the Wolf held up a balled-up scrap of William's tunic. Beddigan took the small bundle and unwrapped it, recognizing the dark, gray, drained chunk of a portal crystal.

Chapter 10: A Most Unwelcoming Welcome

The gravel crunched under Beddigan's boots as he trudged through the forest, nearing the end of his long journey from San Vincent's Port, back to his makeshift home in Windermere. He couldn't stop thinking about William's mysterious disappearance. The entire trip home, his mind just kept turning over the puzzle in his head.

First, William had been shot with some sort of magic by a Lynx sorcerer. Next, he had tumbled over the ship's railing and fell into the sea. And finally, a scrap of his friend's tunic had been found by Captain Marlog, with part of a used portal crystal wrapped in it.

It all seemed too convenient to Beddigan. What were the chances of a piece of tunic ripping free and snagging on a piece of wood from the ship's deck? How had the hearty material even been ripped in the first place, if not deliberately?

And how did a used piece of portal crystal get left behind? Generally, it would have travelled with the user through to the other side. It would have had to have been deliberately tossed back in the few seconds before the portal closed; which meant someone was leaving a clue. Whether that someone was the capturer or William himself remained to be seen. Maybe there was no capturer.

Maybe William had a portal crystal for emergencies and abandoned them to their fate.

But he wouldn't do that! Beddigan thought fiercely, as he strode through the break in the trees and laid eyes upon the shallow valley where the village of Windermere sat, nestled amongst the forest. The brightly coloured roofs stood out stark and welcoming against the backdrop of the evergreen valley.

Beddigan nodded absentmindedly as the villagers greeted him, still lost in thought about the mystery that had ended the enlightening and terrifying trip to the Ranier Islands. Why had the Lynx sorcerers quit attacking? He had assumed it was because the ship was sinking and that the fiends had thought he and Linley, and the crew, were finished. But what if they had something to do with William's disappearance? Had it been that once the Bear was gone, they no longer had a reason to hang around? *Too many questions*, Beddigan thought with a frown as he approached the little house that he and William had called home.

He felt a pang of heartache as he saw that a group of villagers were crowded around the front door. Had they heard that William was missing or dead? He was surprised when they turned to see his approach and met his eyes with not sadness, but fear. The crowd parted and he was taken aback to see the town elder there, waiting for him; a Badger of so many years he rarely left his home.

"Beddigan, I fear that your return cannot be the happy

occasion we had hoped for," the old Badger croaked.

Beddigan furrowed his brow, "I too, have unfortunate news that would preclude any celebration, but what is it that bothers you all so? Has there been trouble in our absence?" he asked.

The Badgers crowded closer, nodding vehemently. The elder leaned in and whispered, "Let us speak elsewhere, lest those we wish not to overhear be privy to this conversation." Beddigan's eyes popped open in surprise again, and he suggested they meet shortly in the common room of Windermere's only guesthouse. Before the Dragon Galantus attacked, the village had been much larger and had housed two more Inns, but they had been badly damaged by Dragon-fire, and had yet to be rebuilt.

The crowd dispersed and Beddigan entered the cottage. After a quick clean up and change of clothing he set out to the guesthouse and was astonished to see how packed it was. *Must be something serious*, he mused as he wound his way through the crowd to a larger table where the elder sat, an empty chair waiting for him. The room grew quiet as he sat down, and it seemed as though every Badger in the village was present, squashed together, turned toward him, waiting patiently.

He cleared his throat, "My goodness, something terrible must have happened," he said, breaking the silence.

The elder Badger nodded gravely, "Perhaps not yet, but we fear our doom is imminent. Something stalks and taunts us in the night. Several villagers have gone missing and then returned with no memory of their absence, and most others are terrorized by something that moves swiftly and silently and has yet to be seen clearly."

Beddigan was listening intently when a young Badger behind him spoke up, cutting off the elder in a most uncommon way,

"But we *have* seen it! Some of us have!" the young Badger yelped. Beddigan turned to see the youth behind him, looking veritably outraged.

The elder frowned, "You've seen nothing, and your imagination runs away with you." The youth held his tongue as the elder continued, "As you can imagine, after being terrorized by that Dragon earlier this turning, some of us are still quite haunted by it."

Beddigan's frown deepened, "You mean to say there have been *Dragon* sightings?" He asked, turning to look at the youth. The Badger still held his tongue but he nodded eagerly, eyes wide with fear.

The elder made a rude noise, "As I said, some of us are haunted by that time, and their minds are drawn to that conclusion. But you have slain the beast, and those who claim to have seen it in the air around Mt. Lileen or swooping over the village at night, would do best to remember that."

Beddigan felt a pit yawn wide in his stomach. He turned back to the youth, "You there, come here," he beckoned. The youth broke through the crowd until he was right next to Beddigan's chair. He leaned in close, "Tell me what you've seen," he said, ignoring the elder's harrumphing.

The youth started chattering excitedly, though fear still showed on his small face, "I saw it! The winged one! I saw his red wings in the sky, and my friend saw it land on the mountain. And I swear I saw it flying above the woods as well!" Beddigan thanked the boy and dismissed him, turning back to the elder.

The elder eyed him with a serious gaze, "Do you really believe another Dragon has chosen to antagonize our little town?" the older Badger asked incredulously. "What would the chances be of that!?"

Beddigan's brow was furrowed, and he waited a moment, collecting his thoughts before he replied. "I think it unlikely, though I am not one to dismiss any account of seeing a Dragon," he said pointedly. "That coupled with the other mysterious incidents the townspeople have been experiencing lead me to believe I should investigate." He stood so that he would be heard more clearly by the rest of the assembled villagers. "I will head up Mt. Lileen immediately and see if I can sort out this mystery that has befallen you all," he said with more boldness than he felt. *And make sure that damn Dragon is rotting in the cave*, he thought as people cheered and thanked him, reaching forward to grasp his paw.

The elder stood, extending his paw to Beddigan, "Thank you, Beddigan, for coming to our aid once again."

Beddigan nodded graciously and shook the old Badger's paw.

"Tell me, what has come of fine William? Surely he would be a help on such a quest..." the elder continued.

Beddigan swallowed the lump that immediately formed in his throat at the thought of his dear, lost friend. He cleared his throat, speaking loudly enough for everyone to hear again, in hopes of not having to repeat himself.

"It is with great displeasure that I inform you that my dearest friend and fellow Adventurer, William Bearhelm, has been lost at sea on our last adventure." A collective gasp made his heart sink further as the room hushed again. "We know not of his whereabouts, but there has been some indication that he may still be alive. I will be investigating, and you shall all be the first to know when I turn something up." Sad nodding Badger faces met his eyes as he looked up.

He forced a small smile, "Hope is not yet lost," he finished.

He met and accepted thanks and compassion on his way out of the crowded room. Once he was back in the sunlight, he assessed the timing of this adventure. If he hurried, he could get up the mountain, remove the caved-in rocks from the entrance, satisfy his growing fear that Galantus was indeed not dead, and still have a bit of light to get down the steeper and more dangerous parts of the mountain.

After a quick stop at his cottage to strap a few extra daggers on, and grab a shovel, he set out for the mountain. He moved quickly, despite the tiredness in his legs from the long trek back to Southern Katheyra. He kept a sharp eye out for anything unusual or suspicious in the forest and through the foothills. Nothing caught his eye as unordinary, which led to him feeling even less comfortable. A sign of something not-Dragon being at fault would have soothed him greatly.

By the time he had scaled the mountain and came to the wide ledge that housed the cave Galantus had called home, he was weary. Every gust of wind that ruffled his fur, brought a tingling on the back of his neck as if he were being watched. When he scrambled up onto the ledge and found that the cave's mouth was still filled with shards of rock from the cave-in, he was most relieved.

The relief didn't last long as a little voice whispered in the back of his mind: *unless there's another entrance.* Shivering involuntarily at that thought, he got to work prying rock shards free with the shovel and tossing them aside.

Several tumbled over the ledge and skittered down to the foothills below. He silently hoped that the villagers were too scared or too smart to have followed him.

As he pried a large boulder free, he set the shovel down, finally able to see inside of the cave. Pulling out his light crystal from the bag on his belt, he affixed it to his leather gauntlet and set it to the brightest setting. He held it up and peered into the darkness of the cave, feeling the pit in his stomach yawn wide as he scanned for what should be at least a partially decomposed Dragon's body. His eyes found only darkness.

"Annalose and Ardra..." he whispered to himself. He started pulling more rock down with his bare paws until the hole was large enough for him to shimmy though.

Once inside the cave, he skittered along the edges of the cavern and turned the light crystal's glow down to a low level. He crept further into the inky black, one paw on the cave wall as he descended far deeper than he had the last time he had ventured into the cave. Bones were strewn about, but otherwise there were no signs of anything living in the cave. He had walked along the curving wall far enough that he could no longer see where he had come in; no sign of light at all.

No sign of anything.

Beddigan continued in the dark, hoping beyond hope that he would not come across another shaft of daylight, and would eventually have to turn back. A dead Dragon who had a disappearing corpse was the mystery he would prefer to solve, rather than an escaped Dragon who now definitely had it out for him.

His heart sank and his gut tightened as he moved around another curved portion of wall and saw daylight begin to lighten the darkness. The cave walls widened into another rounded chamber. A wide mouth looking out over the countryside ended his journey through the mountain.

He moved through the empty room to the cave's opening and skittered to a stop at the edge, realizing there was no ledge on the outside. It was hard to tell from the recess of the cave which direction he was facing, but he could spot the Urkna river in the distance. *Must be a northwestern exit then*, he thought, kicking a rock in frustration. He watched it bump and skid down the jagged rock face.

"Damn this Warbler's Cursed Mountain!" he snarled. His blood turned icy as a rich, velvety laugh erupted behind him.

"My, my, such distaste for my home, Mouse. I cannot blame you though, as I too hate *your* home."

Beddigan turned on his boot heel and sucked in a sharp breath. Hulking in the chamber just behind him stood a Dragon. A far too familiar Dragon; its red wings tucked against its body and the iridescent scales twinkling in the dim light of the cave. The amber eyes watched him with a hint of glee as she stumbled and staggered away from the cave's mouth, assuring some solid rock at his back. The Dragon took a lumbering step towards him, and he drew his sword in a flash of silver.

The Dragon's rich laughter filled the cave again, "I have you now, Beddigan T. Mouze, and you will not escape me."

***

"Scurry all you want, Mouse, you've no escape." Galantus' rich, velvety voice wound through the cavern as Beddigan ran back into the darkness. He cursed under his breath as he felt the ground shake under the Dragon's heavy gait, as it pursued him into the depths of the mountain. He felt the air suck back behind him and ran faster, trailing his paw along the wall of the cave, searching for an alcove, some cover from what he knew was to come. Just as he felt the heat begin to chase him, he found a crack, barely wide enough to slip into and crammed himself in. The roar of fire scorched the wall, and singed the fur on his arm nearest the mouth of the crack. His tail, having not been tucked fully into the crack was scorched as well. He swallowed the pain and slipped out of the crack, into the dark, the acrid smell of burning fur making his stomach turn.

The ground no longer shook with Galantus' steps, so he crept quickly and quietly back to the way he had come. Despite the inky darkness, he kept looking back over his shoulder, expecting to see the light of Dragon-fire once more, or even the Dragon himself at any moment. The passage began to lighten as he approached the chamber of the cave he had entered in. His boot snagged on the ribcage of some unfortunate, long-dead creature and he tripped, falling to his paws and knees on the worn stone of the cave. Rich laughter made his heart grow cold again, as he looked up in the dim light and saw the Dragon's lumbering form appear as if from thin air.

Scrambling backwards he crouched, "Annalose and Ardra!" he gasped.

The Dragon's eyes glinted in the dim light, "Your gods have no place here, Mouse."

Beddigan swallowed the lump that had formed in his throat, taking another step back. *He can turn invisible? I didn't know Dragons had that power*, he thought. The Dragon didn't advance, instead choosing to just watch him with those burning amber eyes. "Funny that it should come back to this chamber. My home, where you set out to destroy me," the Dragon continued.

Beddigan held up his paws in a plaintive gesture, "It was just a job..." he said weakly, mind racing, trying to figure a way out of this mess. *Trapped*, he thought, frustration roiling in his gut. *You utter fool. Coming alone when a Dragon is concerned.*

The Dragon moved a step in his direction, tail whipping around and snagging his feet, sending him falling onto his back. His head smacked the cave floor, his head spinning as he stared up at the stalactites on the ceiling of the cave. Several had come down when he had set the explosion off the first time he had been in the cave, but a few remained. He tucked that detail aside in his mind and rolled quickly out of the way as the large, sharp-clawed foot of Galantus came down, and barely missed squashing him like a bug.

He scrambled along the walls of the cave towards the still partially caved in mouth. Galantus was big, and could breathe fire, but Beddigan was much faster. The Dragon roared and spun, drawing his breath as Beddigan faked left and right, in an attempt to dodge. The Dragon's maw yawned wide and Beddigan doubled back, diving under the beast's chest as fire exploded towards the pile of rock, scorching it with thick black soot. He rolled under the Dragon's arm, and loosed a dagger from his ankle sheath, stabbing it up into the tender, un-scaled flesh of the underside of the Dragon. He was nearly squashed as Galantus roared and whirled, hissing as Beddigan scrambled away again.

"You will regret that!" the Dragon seethed. Beddigan leapt just in time as the tail swooshed around to bat him against the cave wall. With a deep breath and a prayer to every god he knew of, he spun and loosed another dagger which hit its mark, sinking into the flesh on the Dragon's lower neck. With a gurgle and roar of rage, the Galantus advanced quicker than Beddigan could avoid and slammed him against the cave wall, knocking the breath from his lungs. Pinned there by the Dragon's strong tail, Beddigan felt his vision start to get mottled as he struggled to refill his lungs.

The Dragon leaned down, mouth wide in an evil grin, sharp teeth glinting in the dim light, "You are quite the nuisance, Mouse. I had so hoped to char you first before making you my meal, but raw will have to do." Galantus rasped, breath inhibited by the dagger in his neck. Beddigan fought to stay conscious, trying to figure some way to outsmart the Dragon. An idea started to form, but his body was failing. "Any last words?"

Beddigan coughed, fighting for breath, "Dragon... Born," he managed to whisper as his vision went dark. Suddenly he was falling to the cave floor, air rushing into his lungs. They burned as he drew hungry breaths, coughing and hacking; doubled over while his vision slowly came back. His eyes were blurry as he looked up at the Dragon, whose eyes shone, piercing the haze.

"What is it that you know of the Dragon-Born?" Galantus wheezed, shakily.

Beddigan stood on quaking legs as blood rushed back to his appendages. Dragons were rare enough as they are, but the fact that just the word would elicit such strangled curiosity; as if Galantus knew nothing of the small island containing his kin, rocked Beddigan back on his heels. *Valuable information,* Beddigan thought, deciding on how much to reveal. It could save his tail, but at what cost? He didn't know enough about Dragons, Dragon-Born, or their relationship to know if he would be endangering the world to reveal what he knew.

A new plan began to take form, and Beddigan drew himself up to meet the Dragon's gaze, "I happen to know that they exist, which few of us surface-dwellers know for certain. I know they are powerful but weakened in their current state," he said in an even tone, watching the Dragon's reactions as it stiffened, tail moving lazily from side to side as it turned his words over in its head. The Dragon began to move, pacing in the large chamber. Beddigan slid a leather glove free from where it hung tied to the back of his sword sheath and slid it onto his left paw while Galantus was turned away.

The Dragon turned, his eyes on Beddigan, "How am I to know you are not lying, Mouse?"

Beddigan shrugged, though nervous excitement tried to prompt him to move, "You can't be certain."

The Dragon rounded on him, looking closely, "You will take me to them. You will show them to me." Galantus wheezed. Beddigan nodded quickly. Galantus turned away still pacing, "And for this information, I shall spare your life."

Beddigan exploded forward drawing his sword and bounding up the Dragon's back. With a prayer and flying leap, he landed squarely on the Dragon's neck, swinging his sword around its wide girth, grasping the sharp edge with his gloved paw, and pulling back, until the sharp blade dug into the Dragon's flesh. Galantus' roar died quickly as blood started to trickle down his neck. He ducked and shifted, tossing from side to side, and Beddigan hung on for dear life.

"Be still beast!" Beddigan growled as Galantus wheezed and thrashed. "You've terrorized your last town."

Galantus's laughter came out choked as he wheezed, "You are not the only one with information, Mouse."

Beddigan, pulled back on the sword, allowing it to cut deeper into the Dragon's thick flesh. "You cannot trick me, Dragon!"

Beddigan growled.

Galantus' rich chuckle was marred by his wheezing, "Release me if you wish to ever see your dear, Bear friend again."

Beddigan's jaw dropped, and the sword nearly slipped his grip, but he managed to maintain it, easing it back a bit.

"What do you know of William?" Beddigan demanded.

Galantus turned his head so that one of his amber eyes could meet Beddigan's, "Release me and I shall tell you all I know."

Beddigan frowned, "Never trust a Dragon," he echoed words he remembered his father reciting to him many times as a child.

Galantus' chuckled again, "One could say the same for Mice. You have my word, Mouse, but if that is not enough, I will give you one of my scales."

Beddigan tensed. Dragon scales were said to be the strongest substance in all the lands, impervious to all piercing and weight. Along with that, possessing one created some sort of magical shield; the only way to become resistant to Dragon-fire.

Back, long ago when the Dragons were more prevalent in numbers, they were hunted for their scales. Scales were so rare now though that Beddigan couldn't be sure if the lore about them was true.

Galantus sighed and wheezed, plucking an iridescent scale from his side and placed it on the ground. It shone as if it contained its own light source, "Do we have a deal?" Galantus asked, fixing him with his one eye again.

Beddigan weighed his options. He could kill the Dragon, try to find William on his own, and then take the scale, though his sense of right and wrong pushed him away from that path. Instead, he chose to release his sword from the Dragon's neck, and slide down off of its body, boots thumping heavily on the cave floor.

Carefully, keeping the Dragon in his sights, he bent down and picked up the Dragon scale. It was not quite large enough to be a shield, but close. He had seen sketches in history books of the scales mounted onto metal or wood to make a shield of tremendous value.

He stood, meeting Galantus' gaze across the dim chamber, "We have a deal. But if you continue to terrorize Windermere, I will come after you again and again, so do us both a favour and move on!" He said with a snarl.

Galantus chuckled, his voice taking back on its velvety quality again, as the blood on his neck began to clot and dry, "You are a most remarkable Mouse. But yes, I will leave your pitiful town alone."

Beddigan refrained from sighing with relief, though he felt it race through him, "Now what of William?" he questioned the Dragon.

Galantus grinned at him from across the dim chamber, "Your comrade has been taken by the Mormant military."

Beddigan felt the pit in his stomach widen again, leaving him queasy, "No," he whispered, "How do you know this?"

Galantus continued to grin, which thoroughly annoyed Beddigan, "I saw him in their prison pen in Strille. A Bear like him stands out. I was flying overhead, invisible of course, and nearly stopped to pick him up as a snack when I saw him, but figured his punishment would be much worse if he remains in Mormant's clutches."

Beddigan felt sick, thinking of William as a prisoner under the Wolves paws.

Galantus started to move back towards the dark passageway

leading to the other cavern, "Until next time then, Mouse," he said with one last flash of amber eyes and sharp teeth, before he disappeared into the darkness.

Moving woodenly, Beddigan scrambled out of the still partially caved in opening and out into the sunlight. It burned his eyes, causing them to water as he started scaling down the mountainside, acutely aware of how sore and singed he was. By the time he reached Windermere, he was thoroughly exhausted.

Townspeople cheered and ushered him to the common room of the guesthouse where he knew he would be expected to regale the townspeople and the elder with his victory. He slugged ale and mustered up enough energy to give them a rousing story of the battle, leaving out the ending. He was too tired and distracted to even feel bad about lying to them. He did, however, refuse their offer of a fee since he had mistakenly not killed the Dragon the first time, and secretly not killed it the second time.

The townspeople filtered out of the crowded room or went back to their tables once the story was finished, leaving just the village elder and Beddigan at a table together. Beddigan sipped more ale, relishing the feel of warmth that spread through his aching body.

"What will you do next?" the elder asked him.

Beddigan groaned and set down his heavy, pewter mug. He stared at the worn table top for a few long moments before he raised his eyes to meet the elder's,

"I must cross the Lorring Sea, Analose and Ardra save me, and venture into Mormant."

To be continued...

Books In This Series

The Adventures of Beddigan T. Mouze

Volume 2: Across The Lorring Sea

With nothing but hope and some new magical items, Beddigan makes his way across the Lorring Sea, to save his dearest friend. The trip is anything but enjoyable, as plots of war whisper back across the sea to Katheyra.

Volume 3: Over The Snowcap Mountains

On the run, Beddigan and his companions make the treacherous trip over the Snowcap Mountains and into a whole new world. They search for help among the new beings, as the threats of total Wolf domination back home intesify.

About the Author

Mandy Lambert

Mandy has always been an avid reader. Whether it was the high fantasy and romance novels she grew up reading, or the history texts she studied in university, you can pretty much always find her with her nose in a book.

When she isn't reading, she can be found giggling maniacally over administrative work, running around outside like a child (with her children), or watching Star Trek or Sailor Moon and crocheting.